Wanted

Jenn Faulk

Taylor

This place was weird.

Taylor had scarcely allowed himself to think that particular uncharitable thought before his mind was rushing in with an addendum.

Different, not weird. And this place, though it might seem so very different at first, was to be a mission field, a place where God would work through those He'd called here.

Wasn't that what his mother had said to his father, over and over again, when they'd first moved to China as a family and it had been a difficult adjustment? Wasn't that what Pastor Zhao had prayed over Taylor – that he might be a missionary here in the US – before he'd left Shanghai?

Taylor mentally chanted it again as he stepped into the student union building for the first time, taking in the large space, the cavernous lobby, and the crowds of students chatting around tables with takeaway coffee cups in hand, coming out of the bookstore with their arms filled with textbooks, and milling about the space, laughing with each other and texting on their cell phones.

Crowds was a generous term, Taylor thought. There were probably at least a hundred students in this building at the moment, but that wasn't much. Not by Chinese standards.

Different, not weird.

He took a breath, hitching his backpack higher onto his shoulder as he began walking through the building, glancing up at the signage along the way, all the colorful, clashing letters and fonts denoting different restaurants, student services, and office spaces. All of it was in English, which wasn't so unusual, but to see the words *only* in English was unsettling.

The United States was unsettling to Taylor, truth be told.

He should have come here sooner, like his parents had suggested. He should have come back at the end of his last term of school in Shanghai, right after he graduated. He should have come here then and started his college career with a summer term, moving into the dorms early and weathering the extreme culture shock that his parents had known would be his reality. But he'd wanted a few more months in China, some time spent in Chengdu with his brother, a backpacking trip through Guilin with some buddies from school, and one last vacation to Beijing with his parents. America could wait.

And it had. And now he was here.

And he was totally freaked out.

Different not weird, he reminded himself as he found the correct office and made his way inside. Different not weird. And more importantly, this was a mission field, a place where God had directed Taylor, confirming this turn in his path again and again. This college was the right college, a place where God would most definitely use him – odd though he felt – for great purposes, for Kingdom purposes.

The very thought, along with the remembrance of all the prayers his parents had prayed over him throughout the years, leading up to this new season, was a comfort even as he looked around and checked to make sure that he'd found the right office.

Before he could confirm it, the woman at the front desk looked up from her computer and smiled.

"You here for your work study interview, honey?" she asked.

Work study. He'd found it. Thank You, Lord.

"Yes," Taylor said, shifting his bag nervously. "I have a 2:30 appointment with Mr. Jones."

The receptionist, after a few clicks on the keyboard, smiled at him again. "Taylor Robinson?"

"Yes, that's me," he said.

"Mr. Jones is already waiting on you," she said. "First door on the right, down that hall."

Taylor followed her directions, peering around the hallways full of offices as he moved that way, then knocking once on the door she'd specified as he took a breath, opening it up cautiously as a voice inside told him to come on in.

"Taylor Robinson."

The older man behind the desk stood to his feet with the address, smiling warmly over the mess of paperwork strewn from one edge of his space to the other, as he extended his hand.

Taylor took it with a nod and a nervous smile. "Mr. Jones."

"Have a seat," Mr. Jones sighed, dropping back down into his own seat while sifting through some of the papers with one hand and running his other hand through his hair. "I just got your application out a little while ago, and it's… here somewhere. Freshman orientation makes for a mess, especially in the work study office, you know."

"Yes," Taylor said, not sure how to answer this declaration.

But Mr. Jones was moving on, having found the right application and now waving it triumphantly in the air.

"Taylor Robinson," he read out loud, peering through his glasses at the paper. "Let's see what job would be the best fit for you…"

It would be something in the music building, no doubt. Taylor was counting on spending the majority of his time in the music building as it was, eager already to get into the classes that he'd registered for, all entry level music performance classes along with an introduction to music education. It was a very structured program, but he was certain that it would put him on the same road to having a career like his dad, who had been content his entire life to teach music no matter where in the world he found himself. Taylor was similarly interested in that pursuit, but he had an advantage that his father didn't. He could play any stringed instrument completely by ear. It was one of the reasons why his online audition – which included several different instruments – had earned him a spot in the program, along with a hefty scholarship and a work study job option for spending money. All part of God's plan to put him in just the right place at just the right time, his parents had concluded, and Taylor had agreed with them. And the greatest place God could use him would be in the music building, alongside fellow musicians, people who Taylor could relate to in this strange new culture, people who Taylor could share the love of Christ with as he got to know them and began to fulfill his calling to serve God where he was.

It would just make perfect sense for him to work somewhere in the music department, given all of this, given all the great things God was going to do.

Taylor waited for Mr. Jones to say that (about the job, of course, not necessarily about God's calling as this wasn't a Christian college but a wholly secular one), but given the look on the older man's face, that's not what had caught his attention.

"You went to high school in…" Mr. Jones looked down at the application for a confused moment, then glanced back up at Taylor. "Shanghai?"

Shanghai. Even the word brought back flashes of sights, of memories, of warm feelings, and of all that he associated with the city.

Home.

"That's right," Taylor said, reminding himself that it was okay to miss home while still trusting that God had big plans for him here. "Shanghai."

"Shanghai," Mr. Jones repeated.

"Yes."

"But you're not Chinese!"

Well, this was a familiar old tune.

"Unfortunately, I'm not," Taylor said. Unfortunately because he'd certainly always felt Chinese, was more comfortable among the Chinese than Americans, and thought of China as home.

But he wasn't Chinese. He was white. So very, very white.

"Did you grow up there?" the interviewer asked.

"Yes," Taylor said. "For the most part. I moved there when I was twelve, and before that, I was living in a Chinese community in Houston."

His mother had been a missionary to China once upon a time, and when she'd come back home to Houston years ago, she'd planted herself in a Chinese community, continuing to live with the goal of sharing Christ with a people close to her heart. So it had just happened naturally, as she'd married and as she'd had her children, that they'd become a part of that very same community, so much so that Taylor had grown up thinking that he was Chinese.

"That said," he continued, "my permanent address is in China. My parents still live and work in Shanghai."

It was good work. His father taught music at a secondary school in Shanghai, and his mother ran a tour company that catered to mostly Western tourists.

And they shared Christ every day, in every way that they could. Taylor wanted to be like them here at this university, in this small town, in this strange mission field that God had placed him in.

"So, do you speak Chinese?" the interviewer asked.

"I speak Mandarin fluently and can get by with Cantonese," Taylor said.

Mr. Jones just gaped at him, so much so that Taylor felt a little uncomfortable. Like some sort of weird freak, actually.

"Why are you applying for a work study job when you could make some real money as a translator, kid?" the man finally asked, incredulous.

How would he go about that in a town that probably wasn't big enough to have a need for translators? Seriously. Taylor was quite certain that he wouldn't be using any Chinese in this place.

He didn't voice that thought out loud.

"I'm a music education major," he explained instead. "And first year music students —"

"Have really demanding schedules," Mr. Jones said, nodding. "They get you all indoctrinated with those inflexible course loads and all the hours they demand from you that first year. Gotcha."

Indoctrinated. Demand. Well, that all sounded troubling.

"And I guess it wouldn't make sense to look outside of the university for a job when the work study comes as part of your scholarship package," Mr. Jones continued.

"Yes, sir," Taylor agreed, thankful for this understanding and ignoring that indoctrination and demand part for the moment. "It would be better for me if I could find work on campus. And I'm willing to do anything."

Mr. Jones watched him for a long moment, considering this.

"Language skills are helpful," he finally said, going to his computer now and clicking through whatever it was that he was looking at on the monitor. "Even if Chinese isn't a language offered here at the university, a bilingual student is still an asset. And it gives me an idea."

Taylor wasn't sure what this meant.

But did it matter, since Mr. Jones was once again regarding him with a smile? Taylor could feel all of his parents' reassurance about the favor of God washing over him in light of this.

"Kid, I think you might be helpful in the language lab," Mr. Jones said.

"The language lab?"

"Yeah, it's a section of the library where we have computers set up with all kinds of help for the language classes we offer. A section where we need student employees on hand to help out."

"To help out with languages?" Taylor asked, trying to imagine himself in this kind of position.

"More like to help out with the computers," Mr. Jones said. "Someone to help students work the programs so that they can figure out their Spanish, French, and German homework, get some extra assists to supplement what they're learning in class. That kind of thing. It's more about computer applications than actual language skills. But the job requires a bilingual student… even if you're never going to use your Chinese in this job. You still fit the requirement, and we have a shift that's not covered right now."

Taylor nodded at this unexpected turn in his plans. He'd be doing computer work, not working with musicians. But work in a language lab was still work. And it was still a place where God could use him.

That's all that mattered.

"I think that would be a perfect job," he said. "I can learn the software. Easily."

"No doubt," Mr. Jones said. "Because you're going to spend more time doing that than you will actually speaking to students anyway."

Taylor nodded again, just glad for the opportunity to be needed and used, to see what God might do.

"And hey," Mr. Jones said, smiling now as he printed out some papers for Taylor to sign, "you never know. Maybe one day someone will come in, needing something translated in Chinese, huh? And then, there you'll be, right where you needed to be all along."

Maybe. Just maybe.

And even though this place was different – not weird – Taylor felt a little more at home at the thought of being needed, of being useful to Christ, in this mission field.

"I hope so, sir," he said, praying that it would be.

Three Years Later

~Jade~

"I think I want to find my birth mother."

Jade released a relieved breath with the words, praising God that it was out there now. Finally.

She'd never, ever, at any point in her eighteen years been afraid to tell her parents anything. She had friends who regarded their own parents as "them," as near enemies at times, and she'd never been able to understand this. Pulling away and keeping some secrets was probably a natural part of adolescence, loosening the bonds between parent and child, maybe with a little bit of rebellion thrown in there. But that hadn't been the case for Jade. The relationship she had with Mark and Molly Matthews, the only parents she'd ever known, was a transparent one – an affirming, loving, and easy relationship. They prayed together and prayed for one another, something that Jade hadn't always known to treasure, having never known any different growing up. She could share her heart with her parents and always had…

… until this.

It had always been a fascination, this idea of finding her birth mother. A fascination that Jade had only now begun to admit to having, even to herself. She would find herself daydreaming some days, thinking about China, imagining what it was really like from the pictures she'd seen, the videos she'd found online, and the memories her parents had shared with her from their time there, from the one trip they'd made to bring her home eighteen years ago.

Her relationship with her parents was transparent, yes, but here lately, she'd kept this part just to herself, this hope that she had of discovering more about her past… about herself.

And in the back of her mind, the older she grew, she had been surprised to find herself grappling with this notion of connecting who she was and who she would become with the baby who had been left and abandoned, unwanted.

No, Lord, she'd pray just as soon as the thought would linger in her mind. *I'm not unwanted.*

She'd never said it out loud to anyone, not even her parents, just like she'd never said anything to them about finding her birth mother until now. It wasn't self-preservation, the way she'd kept this to herself and not shared it with her parents. It wasn't about her. It was about them, about a need to protect their hearts. Jade knew they could take it the wrong way, that her desire to find her birth mother could be hurtful, could make them assume that they'd been lacking in some way.

That couldn't be farther from the truth.

But Jade watched them now that her admission was out there, nervously glancing from her father to her mother as the two of them looked at one another across the dinner table.

"Okay," her father finally said, slowly and with another glance at her mother. "We can understand that, Jade."

Could they, though?

"It's just natural," he continued on. "That you would want to know about where you came from, about your past."

Jade smiled, thankful for this.

"I was worried," she said. "That you might not understand."

Why, though? They'd understood everything over the years. And in the past few months, they'd been understanding even if it had cost them something, hearing Jade out when she'd made her case for living on campus, for starting her college career in a dorm, even though the university she'd chosen was close enough that she could have commuted from home. They'd not been as protective as most parents of daughters with cerebral palsy would have been, but there was still an understandable hesitancy that was their natural default when it came to letting Jade be independent, even with her limitations. It had been a walk of faith for them to watch her go off to kindergarten years before, still using the tiny crutch that she'd needed from the first time she'd walked on her own in therapy, but they'd done it, even consenting when Jade had wanted to ride the school bus like all of her friends did a couple of years later. They'd been supportive when Jade had grown past needing the crutch and wanted to take ballet, never even flinching when she'd fall at practice and get back up again, her muscles never quite as obedient as the other girls' as they went through their routines. They'd done the same when she'd started high school and joined the marching band, trading in her flute on Friday nights for a flag and an active field routine that she had to work so hard to do, willing her body to do the movements as fluidly as she'd been taught to do them. Her parents had been there, cheering her on through it all. When Jade turned sixteen, they'd continued the process of letting her go slowly, standing in the driveway every time she'd drive away for school or to hang out with friends, waving and praying, no doubt.

And now, she was going to college.

And she was going to find her birth mother.

Her real mother, an ocean away.

"We understand," Molly began, her voice breaking on the second word.

This. This is what Jade had feared, hurting them like this. She reached her hand across the table even as she blinked back tears and grasped her mother's hand in hers.

"Molly," her father sighed.

"Mark, I'm not crying because of me," Jade's mother insisted, holding Jade's hand even tighter, wiping tears away with a napkin. She turned her full attention to her daughter. "I'm crying just thinking of your birth mother, of what she's going to feel when she sees you, when she meets you… I mean, look at you, Jade. Look at what a treasure you are."

Jade had lacked for nothing here in this home. She felt that affirmed again with her mother's response, one that was full of grace and empathy.

"It'll definitely be a moment that God uses for good in her life," Mark said, smiling tenderly at his daughter. "Though I do wonder…"

Jade wiped her eyes now, the tears having come up unexpectedly as she'd been holding her mother's hand.

"What?" she asked. "What do you wonder?"

"How hard is it going to be to find her?" he asked softly, true concern in his voice. "China is a big, big place, you know."

Yes, that would make it slightly different than most searches for birth parents.

"How difficult could it be, though?" Jade's mother cut in. "I'm sure the agency there has the information. And we can go through all of our paperwork from –"

"House of Hope," Jade echoed, smiling as she said the English name of the orphanage she'd been adopted from.

She'd heard the story so many times. Mark and Molly Matthews, married for many, many years, yet childless. A pastor and a school teacher, praying through all of their days for a child of their own, growing disheartened but not desolate because there was always hope. And God had a plan, had put them in the right place at the right time, at a ministry conference where they'd heard a wonderful presentation about international adoptions in China. They'd listened to happy stories from a company that came alongside American families who had a place in their homes for special needs children from China. Mark and Molly had both felt a tug on their hearts, and they'd prayed about it, with God's confirmation coming again and again in the days that followed. So they'd begun the laborious process of adoption, not knowing who it was that they were raising money to bring home, not certain what the medical needs would be, and not even having a definite adoption date to anticipate.

But God had supplied it all in time, along with a picture of a six-month-old baby girl with cerebral palsy in an orphanage in Shanghai. And like that – with just one look – Mark and Molly had new purpose to every step of the process.

Jade had heard the story hundreds of times, about how her parents had gotten clearance to come to China, how they'd gotten to Shanghai after a fourteen hour flight, and how they hadn't wanted to even wait until the next morning to meet their daughter. Oh, they'd been told that there was an adjustment period, that children in these situations were fearful of the strange Westerners, and that not all adoptions went smoothly. There were often tears from parents and children alike, moments of true grief and fear, and the horrible realization that not all parts of adoption were picture perfect.

But this hadn't been the case for the Matthews family.

Maybe it was Jade's age that helped, that she was too young to have heard or understood the wild tales that older children might have told about how the Westerners would come and snatch her away to some horrible unknown. Or maybe it was the way that Mark and Molly came not expecting a moment for themselves, a truly picture worthy moment to share with all of their friends back home, but came to Shanghai wanting only to protect Jade. Or maybe it was the hand of God, working all things out in just the right way, just as He'd orchestrated the binding of hearts across an ocean, around the world. No one could say for sure what it was that made their process so different, but that first meeting was sweet and serene. Perfect. When the workers at the orphanage put Jade in Molly's arms, mother and child breathed a sigh of relief together as though all was right in the world for the first time ever.

"I love you, Jade," Molly had whispered over her, saying her new name to her for the first time. "You are so wanted and so loved."

She'd always been wanted. Jade clung to this truth even now as she thought about China, about the mother who had abandoned her, who had left her behind because she wasn't quite perfect, because she was unwanted.

No, Lord. That's not right…

"House of Hope," Molly repeated now, smiling over at Jade. "We can start there, huh? Do you want your dad and me to do what we can to help you find her?"

And this – her mother's willingness to walk alongside her on this next difficult road – was yet another gift on top of so many others.

"Yes, Mom," Jade said, swallowing past her unexpected tears. "I'd like that very much."

She was checking him out. Totally.

Taylor refrained from shaking his head over her poor judgment and did his best to just focus on doing his job.

"And then, you'll go to that link there to level up to the intermediate studies," he said, trying his best to keep from looking right at her or letting any part of his arm touch her as he pointed to the screen, trying to show her how to navigate the software.

How many times had he said those exact words over the last three years? Too many to count, likely, so much so that it was just second nature, that he could give the instructions to the program without even thinking about the words he was saying.

Every now and then, though, one of these students threw him a curveball.

Like this one today, as she looked up from the monitor in the language lab and gave him a smile, fluttering her eyelashes in what was likely meant to be a flirty movement. She'd probably missed every last instruction he'd given as she'd been gazing up at him adoringly.

"You're so helpful," she said, her voice overly sweet. "It's only the first week of classes, and I'm already behind. So I'll be here a lot. Will probably see you every day."

Taylor let out a tired breath at this, seriously considering warning the girl away from a guy like him.

A guy who was… well, not all that great, honestly.

But instead he just shrugged.

"Whatever," he managed.

He'd changed so much in the last few years. Gone was the idealistic, timid kid who had come to the US thinking that he was on track to pursue a career he'd love, that he'd adjust to life here in a foreign culture easily, and that he'd do great things for God.

God didn't figure into much of anything now. And all of Taylor's plans, much like his life and everything that made him who he was, had been upended long ago.

Wow. Heavy thoughts. And Taylor didn't do heavy thoughts if he could avoid it.

"Okay, well, have at it," he said, gesturing to the screen unenthusiastically before walking away from the bank of computers and heading towards the schedule that was pinned up near the door. He still had a week of work hours to schedule for everyone else – one of the added responsibilities that had come with being promoted to supervisor here. It was a logical promotion as he was the only upperclassmen in this particular work study location, but it was more than that, as Taylor had proven himself to be a hard worker in a job that he hadn't really ever expected or looked forward to back when he'd first started here.

And now… well, now he found himself wondering if he could somehow work it into a real job after graduation.

Yeah, that music education degree he'd been so enthusiastic to start earning as a wide-eyed newbie had quickly become more than he'd counted on, and now that he was in his final year, heading towards graduation, he'd discovered something.

He didn't enjoy teaching. Not like he thought he would, at least. Maybe he'd been idealistic about it all at the beginning, but now that graduation was looming in the not so distant future, he wasn't sure that the reality would live up to its earlier rose-colored visions.

He'd had enough education classes at this point to really make that assessment, the worst of it coming over the past summer when he'd done an internship through the college, teaching orchestra and band camp students alongside other music education majors. The age of the camp participants started at twelve and went through sixteen, and Taylor had discovered in the process that he wanted no part in teaching any age group.

What a horrible time to figure that out, with the end of his degree in sight along with a future of searching for job positions that he didn't want.

It didn't help that his parents both loved what they did for a living and that his older brother was contentedly fast tracking himself through his first year of medical school, studying non-stop and working part-time joyfully towards his dream career. It made Taylor feel as though he'd gotten it wrong somewhere along the way.

What did he want to do with his life? Play music. That was it. But he couldn't make a living doing that, could he?

And as far as getting it wrong somewhere along the way, Taylor was certain that the aptness of that sentiment applied to more than just his education or future profession.

He felt like he'd failed God over and over again. He'd meant to be a shining light for Christ here, but it had been so easy to compromise what he believed and how he lived in order to fit in and find a place to belong in this foreign culture. And as he'd gained friendships and relationships that were as godless as he himself had become, he'd fallen under conviction, remembering who he'd wanted to be initially.

So he'd cut himself off from all of it, from everyone he'd clung to, to the ways he'd lived. At one point, it would have made perfect sense for him to turn back to God in repentance, but Taylor hadn't done so, too ashamed of himself to do much besides retreat into his guilt even further.

And now he was certain that God was done with him, had been done with him for a long while, and would probably never welcome him back ever, never in a million years –

"Excuse me?"

Another student, he thought as he heard the tentative voice, already readying himself to do another quick tutorial on the software, which would be a welcome change from wrestling with his existential crises.

Maybe he should have majored in philosophy. He'd still be looking towards a jobless future, but at least he'd have some vague answers about the meaning of it all.

He finished up his work on the schedule and got ready to do the same introduction and walk through with this student that he always did with first year students. Lots of freshmen had been coming in all week, all of them new to the university, all of them just getting into their language classes –

But all of his thoughts fell silent as he turned towards the voice, his neutral face in place, and finally took her in.

She was definitely not what he was expecting.

He stared for a few silent seconds, his eyes trailing over her in disbelief, then found the power to finally say something.

"Hi."

Lame. But he was shocked – very frankly – at the sight of the girl standing before him. Since coming to this small college town three years ago, he could count on one hand the number of Asian people he'd met. Maybe that said something about this university and its pitiful lack of diversity, something that Taylor had mused on more than once, but it was the reality around here.

Yet here she stood, an Asian student, staring back at him.

And she wasn't just Asian. She was Chinese.

Maybe. Because there was something about her that… that was a little different.

Still Chinese, he assessed as he took her in quickly, feeling his spirits illogically lift as he did so.

Taylor resisted the odd urge he had to reach out and embrace her. But there was something comforting and familiar about her, simply because of her culture alone. How long had it been since he'd seen a Chinese person?

Too long.

"Um… is this the language lab?"

She asked it hesitantly, probably because he was staring at her like an idiot and hadn't said a word.

Taylor noted her accent. She was an American, through and through. But still completely Chinese, all at the same time.

Well… maybe.

"Yes," he finally managed, giving her a smile, something he did so infrequently these days that the very act felt strange and foreign at first. "This is the language lab. Are you taking Spanish, French, or German?"

"Oh, none of them, actually," she said apologetically, adjusting the backpack on her shoulder. "I came by to see if I could find some help translating something I found online. Maybe the language lab has software that translates different languages? I mean, good software, not one of those search engine translators you can find online that jumbles everything up into incoherent nonsense."

"I'm impressed that you know the difference," he said, knowing just what she meant. "Most people don't."

"Well, I may have already tried one of those," she grimaced. "And the translation I got was complete gibberish."

Ahh.

"Well, we specialize in programs that follow along with the classroom work," he said, thinking through the programs and how they were laid out. "No outright translation programs, though that would be helpful."

Really helpful, actually. It wasn't the first time he'd thought it, but given the crestfallen look in this girl's eyes, he thought it again.

"Oh, well," she sighed. "That's okay. I'll figure it out somehow."

"Maybe I can help you look around online, see what I can find?" he asked, not wanting to see her go. Her accent was totally American, not Chinese in the slightest, but still, he felt drawn to her, wanted to help her out.

Which was weird. Really, really weird. He knew this logically, but something about her had him wanting to go above and beyond what he usually did for the students who came here.

"I don't want to pull you away from your work," she said, looking over to the students working at the computers in the room, including the girl he'd been helping earlier who was still staring at him, totally ignoring the French program he'd started for her.

"No, I'd like to help out," he said, gesturing over to the computer at the front of the room, where he sat and did his own work for class, utilizing the computer there when he needed to. "Will you let me?"

And there was that smile again, shy and tentative but still somehow managing to make her whole face glow.

Beautiful.

The assessment surprised him almost as much as the smile that he gave in return.

"Yeah, that would be great," she said. "Thank you."

And she began to walk toward him, limping a little as she did so, so slight that he might not have noticed it if he hadn't been staring at her.

Again.

She noticed the staring as well, looking up at him almost defensively as she neared his desk.

"I'm sorry," he said. "I didn't introduce myself. Taylor Robinson."

He held out his hand, which still felt like a crazy stupid way to greet someone even after all these years in the US.

But it was natural for the girl as she put her hand in his. "Jade Matthews," she said.

Jade.

"You can take my seat," he said, pulling another chair up to the desk as she sat down. "What is it we're needing to translate?"

"The text on this website," she said, pulling out her phone and showing him the browser window she'd opened up.

"Ahh, House of Hope," he read. Then, he stopped himself.

The website was in Chinese. He'd just read it without thinking.

He turned to find that now *she* was staring at *him*.

"Yes, House of Hope," she said quietly. "How did you know that?"

"Well, it's in Chinese," he said. "Excuse me. It's in Mandarin."

She still stared at him.

Oh, he should probably explain it a little better.

"I know Mandarin," he said. "I can read it. Write it. But I speak it much better than I can do the first two."

That was the truth. On those infrequent calls he made home, he spoke with his family in Mandarin, cherishing the easy way it flowed from his lips, not wanting to lose that natural grasp of the language with disuse here in the US.

Jade shook her head, a small laugh escaping as she took in what he'd just said. "I don't know why I'm surprised by that," she said. "I've been praying, after all. It just makes good God sense that I would run into someone who reads Mandarin. That's how He works, you know."

Taylor did know this. He *had* known this, at least.

The way this girl spoke about God and watched Taylor with anticipation, even as the words of praise were breathed out between them… well, it made the hair on the back of his neck stand on end, especially given the thoughts he'd been having earlier.

"Yeah, well," he said, resisting the urge to shake that feeling away. "Sometimes… I guess."

He began pulling the website up on his computer, enlarging the text so that he could read it and translate.

"What are you needing to know about House of Hope?" he said, skimming the words about the Shanghai facility, about the medical care for foster children in the program, adoption waiting lists, and about special needs infants, all of the information filtering through his mind. The dates as well, indicating that the House of Hope website had last been updated fifteen years ago.

Huh. That was troubling.

"I was adopted from House of Hope," Jade said. "Eighteen years ago. And I had some questions about the whole process, how it was handled, some of the background information about it all. I'm hoping to find my birth mother."

But Taylor was still caught up on that first part.

"You were adopted from House of Hope?" he asked. "You were born in China?"

She smiled at this. "Yes, right there in Shanghai."

No way. But… she didn't look Shanghainese. Chinese, yes. But she didn't look like the majority of the people in his hometown.

That, however, wasn't the most troubling thing in what she'd said.

"Are you sure you were adopted from House of Hope?" he asked.

"Definitely," she said, nodding. "My parents have told me about it my whole life."

He looked back at the computer, double checking what he'd read. "But House of Hope was only for children with significant medical issues," he said, looking back at her. "*Very* significant medical issues."

There was nothing wrong with this girl. He instantly felt remorseful at the thought. A medical condition didn't translate to "wrong," of course. But looking over her again, he thought it once more, that she couldn't have been at an orphanage for children who had to undergo difficult and expensive procedures, who would have had extensive hospital stays, and who would have likely been abandoned because those issues were known early on.

This girl was perfect.

The smile she gave him only emphasized that point. "It was House of Hope," she said softly. "I have cerebral palsy."

"Oh," he said, surprised.

"It's why I limp," she said, her eyes meeting his.

He'd almost forgotten about it, but clearly she'd noticed him watching her as she'd been walking.

"It's not as bad as it once was," she said dismissively. "And it's certainly not what they predicted it would be when I was at House of Hope. They told my parents that I'd never walk."

What a grim diagnosis. Taylor looked back at the website, at the blurb that House of Hope had about their children, about their background, and about the gift of adoption.

A gift in more ways than one, he thought, looking back at Jade.

"God is good," she sighed, her eyes on the website. "And He would have been good had I never been adopted, had I never walked. His goodness isn't dependent on my circumstances, of course. But He chose to show His goodness to me by giving me to my parents, who got me to the right doctors, who did the best surgeries, who sent me to physical therapists, who worked with me, who diagnosed medication that helps me manage it all now, and…" She shrugged. "Well, here I am. With a better reality than what was originally diagnosed there in China."

And though Taylor was far away from God himself, something in this resonated deeply with him.

God is good.

"You didn't ask for any of that," she said, giving a little embarrassed laugh. "But to answer your question – yes, I'm sure that I was born in Shanghai and that I was adopted from House of Hope."

He nodded, convinced of the second but not certain of the first.

"Shanghai's my hometown," he said, almost offhandedly as he looked at her, trying to figure out what it was that made her so different from every other girl he'd ever known in Shanghai.

Here as well.

"Really?" she asked, her whole face lighting up. "Are you… you're joking, right?"

"I know," he said. "I'm not Chinese. Unfortunately. But I'm from Shanghai. By way of Houston originally, but I don't count that."

"Why would you," she said, smiling even brighter, "when you could count Shanghai?" Then with a pretty little laugh, "But really… are you being serious?"

"Dead serious," he said, unable to keep from laughing himself. "My parents are still there, in fact."

And his attention went reluctantly back to the website, to the information there.

"And I can't say the same for House of Hope," he said, gesturing towards it. "This website hasn't been updated in fifteen years."

"Wait… what?" she asked, moving forward in her seat, looking with him. "How can you tell?"

"There's a section here about a new initiative they were set to start fifteen years ago," he said. "It says, roughly translated, *coming soon.* And then… nothing."

"And given that, you're concluding that…" She looked up at him expectantly, hopefully.

He didn't want to crush her hopes.

"Maybe it just means that their website is down," he said, bringing up a new browser. "I can search for House of Hope in other places, try a few search engines that aren't blocked in China."

"China blocks sites?" she asked, genuine surprise in her voice.

"Um, yeah," he said. "China's way of protecting its people from the idiocy of Instagram, YouTube, and Facebook, I guess."

But no matter what he searched, he couldn't find any information on House of Hope.

It had likely shut down years ago. And who even knew what that meant for Jade's search and all the questions she had?

He could call some numbers in China. He glanced at his watch, already doing the math in his head, trying to determine what time it was there in Shanghai, when Jade let out a little sigh and turned to him with a disappointed smile.

"We've hit a brick wall, huh?"

He wasn't sure what this saying meant. There were plenty of American sayings he didn't get, but he made a guess at the meaning of this one.

"Not necessarily," he said.

"Likely, though," she said softly, looking at the last page he'd left open, full of Mandarin but no answers.

It was the middle of the night there in Shanghai. Too late to contact most businesses, but he could try later on tonight, early morning in Shanghai –

"I appreciate your help, Taylor," Jade said, before he could offer it. "Thank you for taking the time to help me out."

"I can do more," he said, ready to tell her that he'd get on the phone now, wake his parents up at 3am – no biggie – to see what they could find on their end. Even if he couldn't call businesses or government offices at this hour, he could still do something.

"You've done so much just by caring enough to try," she said, putting her hand on his arm for just a brief second. "Thank you for that."

The kindness there in her eyes – the genuine goodness and kindness – took him by surprise. People weren't this good. There was something about this girl, something godly and pure.

Something that meant she should stay far, far away from him.

"I've got to get to my two o'clock class anyway," she said, standing and picking up her backpack.

"You've got time," he said, glancing at his watch again, noting that the first of the afternoon classes wouldn't start for another twenty minutes.

"It takes me a little longer to get across campus than it takes most students," she said. "But that's okay."

He could get her number, then. Call her later tonight after he'd made some calls to Shanghai himself –

"Thank you again, Taylor," she said.

And something in the way she proudly picked up her backpack again and began her slow, unsteady walk toward the door kept him from uttering another word.

She was strong and good, godly and pure.

And she didn't need to be hanging around him.

~Jade~

"What did I miss?"

Jade looked up from her flute case and smiled at Olivia, one of her suitemates from the freshman dorm.

When she'd made the decision to move into the dorm, Jade had begun to pray that God would give her Christian roommates, girls who could be her close friends, who could spur her on in godliness, who she, too, could hold accountable.

And God said no.

Kimberlyn, her roommate, had a boyfriend who lived in an off campus apartment, and she spent most of her weekends and her weeknights with him, coming back to the dorm only to pick up more of her stuff and to occasionally study. And Marley, one of her suitemates, had pledged a sorority and spent almost all of her time flitting from one event to another, only crashing late at night in the dorm. It hadn't taken Jade long to discover that neither girl was a believer, but she'd counted it as providential that God had arranged it all just so, as she was quickly becoming friends with both of them and prayed that she would be an encourager to them, a light pointing them to Christ she prayed, as she loved them and cared for them.

And then there was Olivia, her other suitemate. Olivia, who wasn't a Christian either, but who was a music major and an avid anime fan. She'd taken one look at Jade on move-in day and exuberantly concluded (erroneously) that Jade had to be into anime as well because she was Japanese. Jade had gently corrected her on both fronts with a smile and without any hard feelings (because she was always getting confused as being any number of Asian ethnicities), and that might have been the end of their potential friendship. But Olivia saw Jade's flute case and was off on another over the top tangent.

"Are you a music major, too?!" she'd exclaimed, taking Jade's hands in hers and all but twirling her around in a circle. "We'll have the same classes! I'm a woodwind player, too! Clarinet!"

Jade had clarified that she wasn't a music major, just a flute player hoping to fulfill her fine arts credit with a couple of semesters of a freshman woodwind ensemble class. That had been enough for Olivia, though, who had been delighted to find that they were in the very same section.

Being in the same class with Jade was especially helpful on the days that Olivia was kept late in her introduction to music theory class, arriving just in time to put her clarinet together and asking Jade if she'd missed anything in all of the pre-class drama and gossip.

"You didn't miss a thing," Jade said to her as they both began putting together their instruments.

"That's a pity," Olivia muttered around her reed. "I heard that *Crenshaw* was going to be late, and I was hoping there was some really great story behind it. Like she got attacked by wild dogs."

Jade shook her head at the way Olivia had said the name of the TA leading their ensemble class. Crenshaw wasn't that bad. Maybe a little too high on her own power at times –

No, Jade wouldn't think negatively about her. Everyone had their issues, their worries, their pains, and their disappointments. Jade understood that better than most, especially since none of her attempts to find out more information about her adoption or the House of Hope had ended with any major leads. The language barrier was a huge deterrent, and the calls her mother had made to the embassy to see about obtaining Jade's records in China had resulted in being put on hold, on leaving messages, and on being told to wait for a call back.

"Well, good gravy," Molly had said just a couple of days earlier with a great, dramatic breath. "Who would have thought that getting answers would have involved nothing short of an act of international diplomacy?!"

Jade had just sighed, discouraged and crestfallen. "I can't believe we've never had a need for any of my documents before now."

"We got your certificate of birth abroad, your social security card, and your passport just as soon as you were legally ours," Molly had said. "And we were told that was all you would ever need. Who knows what adoption in China looks like now, but that was the situation back when we were there."

It had been. And those documents had been enough… until they weren't enough to tell Jade anything about her past.

"I'm going to keep on calling and searching," Molly had said, determination in her words. "Even if I end up having to go to China myself to get some answers!"

Jade smiled even in the rehearsal room as she thought of her mother's perseverance, a perseverance which would certainly lead her to continue on long past the point where it would actually help. While her mother hadn't yet given up, one closed door after another had left Jade concluding that maybe… well, maybe this just wasn't going to happen.

She would continue to be patient, to pray that God would work it all out at just the right time.

"You ever wish there were more guys in this class?" Olivia said to her before effortlessly playing a quick scale on her clarinet. "It's like no man's land in every single woodwind ensemble class on this campus. I mean that literally, Jade."

"I hadn't noticed," Jade said honestly, looking around as well. "What about that saxophone player —"

"That's a woman, Jade," Olivia said, peering back there as well. "I think."

"Well, not that it matters," Jade said, turning her attention back to the front, anticipating that Crenshaw would storm in at any moment, demanding that they turn to their first piece of the day and begin before any of them could hardly catch a breath.

"Your chemistry classes any better?" Olivia asked in between scales, warming up. "Is it raining men over there?"

"I'm the only girl in a good portion of my classes," Jade said honestly. "And the only female pre-pharmacy student."

"Go on with your bad self, pill popper," Olivia said. "And while you're at it, find me a nerdy, pill popping man to —"

But whatever she'd been readying herself to say was cut short when the door opened. Instead of Crenshaw storming in, fit to put them all through the ringer because she was in a mood, someone very different walked in.

Someone Jade recognized instantly.

"Forget finding me a nerd, Jade," Olivia whispered. "I want this guy."

This guy. The guy from the language lab. The guy from Shanghai.

The Chinese guy, who… well, wasn't Chinese at all.

Taylor Robinson.

The very thought of their conversation in the language lab made Jade smile, just at the same moment that his eye caught hers.

There was recognition there in his gaze as well as he stood in front of their ensemble class, a paper in his hands.

"Hey," he said, not to the whole room but just to her.

And Jade felt like every set of eyes in the room turned to her for a brief moment, before the guy spoke again.

"Hey, I'm Taylor," he said to the whole class, rubbing the back of his neck and looking down at the sheet. "One of the music education professors sent me over here to get you all started while we wait for your TA." He continued studying the paper. "Who is your teacher?"

"Crenshaw," Olivia bellowed in a deep, ominous voice as though their TA was some dangerous monster.

And perhaps she was, Jade thought, as a concerned expression crossed Taylor's face.

"Mindy Crenshaw?" he asked.

Crenshaw had a first name? And Mindy. What a happy name for such an unhappy person.

Jade felt guilty for even having the thought.

"Scary, wicked oboe player?" Olivia asked Taylor. "That Crenshaw? One in the same, my friend."

Taylor swallowed, looking towards the door with dread in his eyes.

"How about you?" Olivia kept on. "Are you a TA? Music education major? Let me guess – you teach the drummers."

Jade was glad for her friend's inability to keep quiet, curious to hear the answers herself.

"Uhh, yeah," he said. "TA, music education. But I teach the bluegrass section."

"Bluegrass?" Olivia said, grinning. "We have a bluegrass ensemble? I'm not even sure what instruments are included in that –"

Her words were cut off when Crenshaw stormed in, harried and hurried and even more irritated than normal.

And then, she saw Taylor.

"Just great," she muttered, putting her bag, her oboe case, and all of the folders down with her back turned to him, rolling her eyes as she did so. "The great Taylor Robinson. And I see that you've done nothing to get my class started."

He hadn't had a chance with all the questions Olivia had been volleying his direction.

"I'll let you handle it," he said, putting the paper down on the podium, doing his best to not meet the glare that Crenshaw was shooting his way.

"You just do that then," she snapped at him.

And Taylor, after exchanging one last hopeful glance with Jade, walked out.

Olivia nudged her, and when Jade looked her way, there was an obvious question in her eyes.

A question that Jade didn't have time to answer even if she'd had an answer to give, as Crenshaw stepped up to the podium, making them sit up straighter, their hands ready to quickly shuffle to the first music piece she called out, their breaths held.

But Crenshaw looked out at them all with thinly veiled annoyance, a philosophical tone in the words she uttered. "Just a word of advice, ladies. There are men in this department that you'll all want to steer clear of. And guys like him?" She nodded her head towards the door. "The love you and leave you kind? Are the type you'll want to avoid completely."

The love you and leave you kind.

Jade looked that direction as well, thinking about Taylor, wondering about Crenshaw's words.

But there wasn't time to think too deeply about it because Crenshaw was soon barking orders. She was particularly ruthless during the rehearsal, so much so that Jade, who enjoyed playing music and could rehearse for hours, still wanting more, found herself glad on this particular day that Crenshaw only had an hour and a half of time to subject them to her own personal conducting torture.

"I'm glad that's over," Olivia whispered close to Jade's ear as they edged past the angry TA and blessedly left the room. "That woman seriously needs to reconsider what she's doing with her life."

"Everyone has a hard day now and then," Jade said, her mind still troubled with the recollection of Crenshaw's words regarding Taylor Robinson.

Taylor Robinson, who she noted after Olivia began frantically nudging her, was sitting there in the lobby of the music building, standing to his feet as his eyes met hers.

Jade stood still for a minute, both Olivia and Taylor staring at her, before she finally found her voice.

But she wasn't the one who spoke first.

"Jade," Taylor said. "Can I talk to you?"

He'd been thinking about Jade Matthews and her situation.

It had been a few days since she'd come by and he'd learned about House of Hope. While Jade hadn't left him any more information to go on or consider, seemingly giving up when they'd encountered problems with the website, Taylor hadn't been able to do the same.

He'd called his parents the same day, going through their regular pleasantries – the easy back and forth of checking in on each other just like they always did, always in Chinese – when he abruptly changed the subject.

And he'd started speaking English as he'd done so, wanting nothing to be lost in translation on the subject.

"Have you ever heard of a place called House of Hope?" he'd asked his mother. He'd rattled off the address he'd found when he'd gone back and rechecked the old website after Jade had gone on, leaving him behind.

House of Hope was surprisingly close to where his parents lived, in the very same section of Shanghai where his father taught, just a few blocks over from his mother's office.

"House of Hope," Hannah Robinson had repeated. "Never heard of it. What is it?"

"It's an orphanage in Shanghai," he said. "Or it was, years ago. And I'm not even sure that orphanage is the right word. From what I've been able to glean from their old website, it was more like a foster home, a place where children with special needs stayed when they were in and out of hospital care, when they were waiting to be adopted by foreign families."

Hannah hadn't said anything for a long moment, mulling all of this information over. "Okay… why are we talking about this?"

"There was a girl who came into the language lab today," he said, running his hand through his hair as he paced with his phone held to his ear, back and forth in his tiny off-campus apartment where he had sheet music spread out in piles, his guitar, his yueqin, and his banjo on stands near the threadbare couch. "She was adopted from House of Hope. And she's trying to find her birth mother."

"Wow," Hannah had sighed. "Does she know that's going to be like trying to find a needle in a haystack?"

"Right?" Taylor had echoed. Then, he thought about it. "Well, actually… I don't know. Is it going to be any more difficult than it would be to find a birth mother here in the States?"

He had no idea how adoption in China worked. In the US, there was a clear system linking birth parents to adopted children, even if those files were sealed. Yet still, it wasn't always an easy process. And even with a population that was so much smaller than China, the search would still be laborious.

Taylor thought through all of this before his mother could even say the words.

"I think it'll be more difficult than finding out the details of a stateside adoption," she said. "But this young woman has a starting point, at least."

"She would," Taylor continued on. "But House of Hope doesn't appear to still be up and running."

"Give me that address again, Taylor," Hannah had said, and he had repeated it to her. "I'll check into it. See what I can find on my end."

Just what he'd hoped she would say.

Then the conversation had moved to the newest piece of family news, with his dad getting on the line as well and telling him all about it.

"Pandas?" Taylor had repeated, making sure he'd heard clearly. "Hudson is working with pandas?"

"I think he's shoveling poop at this point," Owen Robinson replied gleefully. "But he's got his foot in the door, so I'm sure in no time at all he'll be dealing directly with the pandas himself. You know him. Went in and charmed whoever it was who could get him an entry-level position there. And I'm not sure how he's fitting it in with his classes and his internship with the genetics department at the university. But he's doing it."

Of course he was. Because Hudson had been driven all through high school towards a higher goal – becoming a veterinarian with a focus on large mammals and breeding endangered species – and hadn't veered away from it all through college, which he'd completed earlier than most students by taking on more courses each term and never having a break that didn't include at least a few hours of classes that would count toward his degree. His Mandarin was fantastic, but it was nothing compared to his abilities when it came to science and math.

No wonder he was on course to walk right into his dream job in a few years, even if he had to wade through (and shovel) some panda poop on his way there. He was probably thankful for even that, counting it as good research to study their excrement as he went about his work.

"We had to take a trip out to Chengdu to pick up Ling," Hannah said. "Apparently there are rules about panda keepers not having pets. Something about bringing potential diseases to the pandas?"

"I don't know," Owen cut in. "But we've got Ling now. Had to pay a fortune to fly him on the plane in the cargo hold. And we have to brush his hair multiple times a day. I swear, he's the most high maintenance dog ever."

Taylor had smiled at the thought of his brother's Chow and at the mental image of his dad brushing out the pampered dog's long coat every day.

"But going out there gave us some time to speak face to face with Hudson," Hannah said, excitement in her voice. "And hear about the big things that are happening there with his circle of friends." There was a long pause, and Taylor could have sworn that he could see his parents smiling at one another. "Big Kingdom things."

They had to speak in nuanced ways about his mother's real work in China, the work of sharing the gospel and making disciples.

But Taylor heard them loud and clear.

Hudson was sharing Christ with his classmates and his fellow workers. He was planting a church.

Of course he was. Was there anything his older brother couldn't do?

"Well, good on him," Taylor said.

"He's right where he needs to be," Hannah said. "As are you, Taylor."

He was here, far from God, nothing like his brother, nothing like who he'd been when he'd left China years ago.

"We're thinking about you," Owen spoke up.

This was nuanced as well. They were thinking about him, praying for him.

"I know," he said, thinking that their prayers hadn't amounted to much, only more guilt on his part and a greater need that he felt to distance himself from them, which sadly meant that he was farther from China. When he'd first come to the States, he'd envisioned going back home as often as he could with his schedule and the expenses, but after freshman year had gone the way it had, he no longer even thought about going back home.

He hadn't been back to China in three years.

It was better for everyone this way. His parents could never know how much he'd fallen, how far away he was from God now.

But maybe they had an inkling, if the way they kept reminding him that they were thinking of him was any indication.

"And we'll be thinking about this girl you mentioned," Hannah said. "What a great coincidence, huh? She needed information about China, and there you were, waiting for her."

His mother didn't believe it was a coincidence any more than Jade herself had that day. Hadn't she told him that it was a great God thing, that he'd been there when she needed him?

He'd doubted it then. He doubted it on the phone with his parents. He even doubted it when his mother had told him she'd look into it.

But he began to wonder when she got back in touch with him the next day with a couple of promising phone numbers. He hadn't been sure how he was going to find Jade, and then, there she had been, in Mindy Crenshaw's class of all places.

He didn't mind filling in when needed, but Mindy Crenshaw was someone he tried to avoid. There was some bad blood between them, stemming from some poor decisions he'd made his freshman year, and seeing her only tended to make him feel worse about himself.

And he was feeling pretty low as he waited for her class to end, but he continued waiting there anyway because he needed to speak with Jade about the numbers he'd found.

He could just give them to her and be done with it. But what was she going to do — call these two people who had at one time been connected to House of Hope and have a broken English conversation about the dates and details of her adoption, asking for answers that likely weren't clear in any language? No, he couldn't just give Jade the number. He'd need to call on her behalf and have these conversations in Mandarin, but he would need her there in case there were questions they asked that he couldn't answer.

He felt compelled to do this for her. And even the feelings that Mindy Crenshaw had brought up in him with just a look that communicated the totality of his worth couldn't deter him from doing this one good thing.

Helping Jade.

Jade, who stood next to another girl, a girl who was nudging her closer to him very deliberately.

"Jade," he said, moving to go and stand with her. "Can I talk to you?"

Her friend nudged her even more, so much so that Jade shot her a look, which had the friend dramatically looking at her watch.

"And look at that," she said. "It's time for me to get across campus for a history class. Catch you later, Jade."

The girl gave Taylor a flirty wink just as she was turning away.

But from Jade, there was just a cautious smile, that same look of kindness that she'd worn earlier when he'd spotted her in the rehearsal room, as though God had placed her right in his path at just the right time.

Did he believe that God could do those kinds of things? Absolutely. Did he believe that God would do those things for him? No, not anymore. He didn't deserve that kind of favor.

But maybe Jade did.

This reminded him of the numbers he had, the whole reason that he was here waiting for her. God had shown her favor already, in giving them a trail to follow.

Them, as if he was part of her search as well. But he was, wasn't he? Ready to see it all through with her.

"Hey, Taylor," she said, smiling at him. "What did you want to talk about?"

"I called my parents," he said. "You know, in Shanghai."

It was entirely possible that she'd forgotten all about their conversation, that she'd written him off as soon as it was clear that he couldn't help her.

But that wasn't the case. He could tell as she smiled.

"Yes, of course," she said. "I remember. How could I forget that? You're the first Chinese person I've ever met."

She smiled wider at this.

He couldn't keep from smiling as well.

"That's… that's very sad," he said, still grinning.

"Why is that sad?" she asked, giving a little laugh on the last word.

"Because I'm not Chinese," he said. "And the thought that you've been alive for eighteen years –"

"Almost nineteen," she said, grinning even more.

"Okay, you're almost nineteen" he smiled, "and you've never met anyone who looks like you…"

He'd never met anyone who looked just like her either. Yes, he'd met plenty of Chinese people in his lifetime, obviously, but he'd never met anyone as beautiful as Jade was when she gave him that smile.

Pity that. And what a strange thought to have.

"Well, yes, maybe that is sad," she said, conceding to that. "But meeting you hasn't been sad at all. Because now I have one Chinese friend in this world."

Friend.

He knew next to nothing about this girl, but that word touched his heart. Friendships had always been hard to come by here with how out of place he felt. And when he'd been popular his freshman year because he was living like everyone else, there had been people around him all of the time.

But none of them had been true friends. And while some of them, like Mindy Crenshaw unfortunately, had decidedly declared him an enemy since then, most had just walked away and become strangers in the crowd.

A friend.

He nodded at Jade, at the endearment. "Well, like I said, I talked to my parents, and my mom found a couple of names of some people who were connected to House of Hope."

Jade gave a sound that was somewhere between a gasp and a laugh. "Did she? Really?"

"Really," he said, nodding. "And she got their numbers so that we can call them, chat with them, see if they were there at the right time, and find out what they know about records, about what we can do next to find your birth mother."

There were tears in her eyes as she listened to this.

And before he could say anything else, either tell her not to get her hopes up or promise her that they were getting close to some answers, she put her arms around him in an unexpected hug.

"Thank you, Taylor," she said, tears in the words.

And Taylor found himself inexplicably emotional as well, standing in the music building lobby, holding his new friend in his arms.

Taylor hadn't forgotten about her.

In all that he had going on and all that he likely had to do as an upperclassman, he'd remembered her and the details she'd given him about House of Hope.

This was extraordinary, especially given what she now knew about him, that he was a music education major, that he not only had his own classes to attend but also a work study job and responsibilities as a TA for an ensemble section.

Bluegrass.

That was the first thing she brought up early the next morning when they met inside the student union building, so early that just the coffee shop was open.

"Bluegrass?" he'd repeated, handing her a coffee cup, just as soon as she'd asked the question and sat down next to him on one of the couches in the lobby. "What about it?"

"You teach it," she said, accepting the cup. "And thank you, by the way. I should be treating you, given that I'm the reason you're here so early, that you're doing any of this."

"My pleasure," he said, taking a sip from his own cup. "And I had to have something to wake myself up. Musicians tend to keep late hours, you know."

"Bluegrass musicians," she said, smiling around her cup. "What instruments do you play?"

"Um, well," he said, sighing, as if he had to think about it, "guitar, obviously. The mandolin. And I love the banjo. I can manage on a violin. The sanxian. The pipa and liuqin. But my favorite of all is the yueqin."

She blinked at him, not sure if she should recognize the latter half of those instruments. "The yueqin?" she asked.

"It's a Chinese instrument," he said. "As is the sanxian, the pipa, and the liuqin. All stringed instruments. Not bluegrass, but if you can play one…" He shrugged. "You can usually play them all. Or maybe not. I don't know. But I can."

"That's awesome," she said appreciatively, grinning. "And I would imagine that takes skill. That playing one stringed instrument doesn't make it a certainty that you can play them all. You must be especially gifted in order to do that, made just so for some big plans that God has for you."

Now he blinked at her, seemingly uncertain what to do with this.

"I play by ear," he offered. "My grandmother did, too. The piano, at least."

"That must be incredible," Jade sighed enviously. "Able to just pick it up and do it. The flute doesn't come naturally to me at all, but I enjoy it. And it's a great way to take care of my fine arts credit."

"So you're not a music major?" he asked. "I wondered when I saw you in… Mindy's class yesterday."

Crenshaw. The words Crenshaw had said about him went through Jade's mind briefly.

The love you and leave you kind.

"No," Jade said, smiling despite this, not wanting to make judgments on anyone because of someone else's words. "I'm a chemistry major. Pre-pharmacy."

Taylor raised his eyebrows. "Wow. So you're smart."

Jade gestured towards her face. "Well, of course I am. I'm Asian. Duh."

He looked a little shocked at this.

She laughed out loud. "Oh, come on," she said. "Asian girl in a white girl world. I can make those kinds of jokes, right? And maybe there's something to that horrible stereotype because yes… I am smart." She grinned wider. "And God had certainly given me a natural inclination towards pharmaceutics, since my cerebral palsy has made me something of an expert on certain types of drugs. All God appointed."

Taylor looked doubtful at this, uncertain of what to say.

Jade kept right on talking. This was her favorite thing to share with people. And Taylor had likely thought about it anyway. Wasn't that what people always thought when they met her? Wondering about her disability? No wonder. It had likely been the reason she'd been unwanted all those years ago in China –

No, she wasn't unwanted.

"It's like that story in scripture," she said, pushing past this and reminding herself of real truth even as she shared it with him. "The one about the man who was blind from birth. Everyone was asking Jesus the wrong questions. Whose sins made this happen?

Was the blindness the man's fault? Was it his parents' fault that he was born blind? Who was to blame? And Jesus told them very plainly that it was no one's fault. He said, 'But it was so that the works of God might be displayed in him.' And then, of course, Jesus healed him. He hasn't healed my cerebral palsy, obviously, but the principle applies even still. I'm this way so that the works of God might be displayed in my life. And I figure one of those ways will be through my own future ability to make life easier for others like me, using chemistry and medication to do so."

He hadn't asked for any of that, yet she'd offered it. She always did with people. There was nothing to feel sorry about when it came to her condition, to her adoption, to any of it.

God would work it all out for good. He already had.

"That's a great way of looking at it," Taylor said.

"Probably the same way you look at your musical gifts," she said, taking another sip of coffee.

She wasn't sure given the uncertainty in his eyes.

"And given your language skills," she said. "I'm absolutely certain that God equipped you with those for this moment in time."

"I think you may be right," he sighed, pulling his phone out. "And speaking of, this is a great hour to call Shanghai."

Shanghai. Oh, she could feel herself getting excited at the very word.

"I don't know how you want to do this," he said, glancing over at her. "Speakerphone?"

"Yes, please," she said. "I want to hear everything."

He nodded, then went to his text messages and touched one of the numbers listed on one of his texts.

It was just that easy.

It hadn't been that easy, obviously, but Taylor made it look easy, turning the speakerphone on as the phone rang, looking up at her encouragingly, just as a man answered.

Then Taylor began to chat with him.

In Chinese.

So much for being a smart Asian girl. Jade giggled to herself as the conversation continued on, tickled that when she'd told him to use the speakerphone (because she wanted to hear everything) that she hadn't realized that she wouldn't understand a single word.

Oh, but she was still enjoying listening to Taylor talk, even as he looked up and gave her a crooked smile as she did her best to muffle her laughter. On and on he went, the sound of his Mandarin strange and unusual, foreign and soothing and melodic.

"Jade," he said a few minutes in. "What was your exact adoption date?"

"Oh, here," she said, pulling the information up quickly on her phone. Her birthday. Estimated, at least, since they couldn't be certain. And her official adoption date.

That was it. That was all the information Jade had about the first part of her life.

Taylor looked at it and smiled. "That's my birthday, too, Jade. Well, three years before yours," he whispered.

That made her smile as well.

Then Taylor switched back to Chinese, giving the man on the phone the dates. And after listening for a long while, he grimaced. More words, as Taylor sighed and looked up, nodding in understanding.

He hung up and looked at her.

"Bad news?" she asked.

"No news," he said. "That particular gentleman wasn't a part of House of Hope by the time you came around. He left three years earlier for a job in Taiwan and couldn't tell me who was even running House of Hope when you were there."

Oh.

"But my mother found two names," he said encouragingly. "And I can try the second right now."

"Thank you, Taylor," she said.

"Do you want the speakerphone on for this one, too?" he asked, smirking a little. "Even though you didn't get any of that?"

"Hey, maybe I understood every single word," she said, unable to keep from laughing. "Maybe my Mandarin is coming back to me even now, the language of my infancy still back there in my subconscious."

"Don't say that," he laughed back. "If you start speaking Mandarin on your own, you won't need me."

"No, I will," she said. "Need you, that is."

And he smiled at this, touching the next name, putting the conversation on speakerphone.

At first, Jade couldn't tell what was happening with the beeps and a voice, speaking what sounded like a pre-recorded message.

Sure enough, that's what it was as Taylor mouthed the word – voicemail – to her, right before he gave another sigh then started speaking.

Then, he hung up.

"Did you leave a message?" she asked.

"I did," he said. "We'll see if they get back with me."

"But you didn't give them your name," she said.

"I did," he corrected her. "I gave them my Chinese name."

She grinned. "Taylor is a Chinese name? Or has a Chinese equivalent?"

"It most certainly isn't a Chinese name," he said, smiling as well. "But there's a word for it, thanks to Hudson Taylor."

She sat up straighter. "Hudson Taylor," she said. "I know all about him!"

She'd heard stories her whole life about missionaries to China. Lottie Moon, Liang Fa, John Sung, Gladys Aylward, and of course, Hudson Taylor. Her parents might not have been able to always translate Chinese culture to her in their small town, but they'd always given her stories about great movements of faith in China.

"Are you named after him?" she asked. Then, before she could stop herself, "Are you a Christian?"

"Yeah," he said, a little hesitant. "I'm named after him. And my brother… he's named Hudson."

She didn't miss that he hadn't answered her second question, but she was too delighted by the names to linger on it.

There would be time to ask him about it later, maybe share more with him if he was uncertain about where he stood with God.

Yes, she'd wanted to be a missionary to China once upon a time, after hearing all of those great stories of the faith. And she still had a missionary's heart.

What a funny twist. An American Chinese-born girl, sharing Christ with a boy named after Hudson Taylor.

"Hudson and Taylor," she sighed appreciatively. "That's what you and your brother are named?"

"It is."

She grinned wider. "Your parents must be fun people."

He laughed out loud at this. "Well, they're not very original, that's for sure. But yeah… they're fun, I guess."

"And they're in China because…"

Because of their faith. Because they were yet two more heroes of the faith, missionaries to China, just like the ones Jade had heard about all of her life. But they probably couldn't say it, couldn't be obvious about it, because China…

She could see the unspoken words there in Taylor's gaze.

"Yeah," he sighed. "Something like that."

Then why was he clearly uncomfortable regarding questions about faith?

"So what's your Chinese name?" she asked instead, sensing his unease.

And he told her, making her smile even more.

"And Jade?" she asked. "What is Jade in Chinese?"

He told her that, too, after hesitating for a moment.

"What?" she asked. "Do people not talk about jade in China? Do they not say the word often?"

Jade was a gem. She knew this. She'd never owned any herself, but she knew about it, knew that its connection to China was why her parents had picked it when they were deciding on her name.

"They talk about jade," he said. "They're very proud of jade in China. They actually have a saying about it. That's what I was thinking of when you asked for the Chinese name."

"What do they say?" she asked.

After a long pause, he told her.

"Gold is valuable, jade invaluable."

Invaluable. Not unwanted.

And Jade wasn't sure why this saying felt like an assessment straight from the heart of God, especially coming from a man who seemed to be estranged from Him.

But it did.

Straight from the heart of God. Valuable. Wanted.

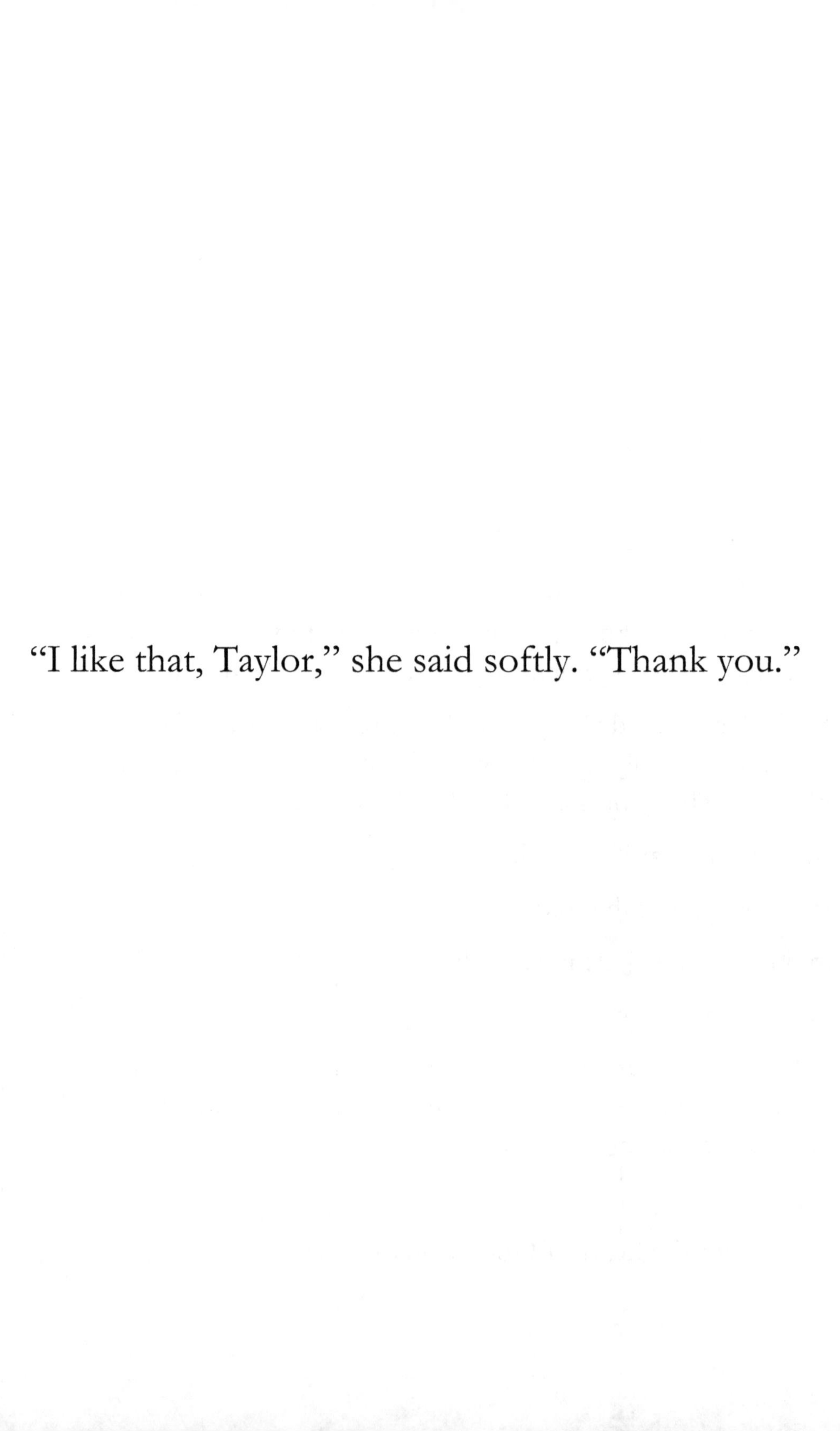

"I like that, Taylor," she said softly. "Thank you."

Jade wasn't easily discouraged.

When neither call on that early morning went anywhere, Taylor had expected that she'd be down about it, that she would understand the gravity of the situation of not having any other leads.

But even after those dead ends, she'd just shrugged and smiled.

"I appreciate your help," she said. "I wish there was something I could do to repay you for your time."

He'd shaken his head at this. "I feel invested in it now, too. Like it's a great mystery we've got to solve."

A great mystery. What happened with House of Hope? And who was there back when Jade had been born?

He was invested in it now. And while he couldn't pinpoint exactly why he felt that way, he knew he was going to see this through to its conclusion, right beside Jade.

She'd smiled at this. "Well," she said, "I'm praying that you hear from that second guy, that he calls you back and has a good answer."

Taylor wasn't one for praying much, but he nodded at the sentiment anyway, knowing that if God was listening to anyone's prayers, He'd certainly be listening to the prayers of this godly woman. What she'd said about God using her cerebral palsy for His glory spoke volumes about the way she saw Him, saw herself, and understood the world. Something about it had resonated with

Taylor, long after the two of them had said goodbye that day and as Taylor had told her he'd be in touch if he heard back from the second caller. Or even if he didn't.

He'd figure something out.

The longer he and Jade chatted that morning, the more determined he was to make something happen for her. She was genuinely good and kind, asking him all kinds of questions about his music, about his job at the language lab, and about his parents' work in Shanghai.

She'd been very interested in that, and he'd told her some of the stories his mother always did, about her life long before marriage, when she'd been on the mission field in China, single and able to go anywhere and do anything.

"That's exciting," Jade said, sighing. "That kind of freedom. Takes guts, too."

"Maybe," Taylor had said, thinking that it had never sounded that way to him. "My mother's grandfather – my great-grandfather – was a missionary, too. To Namibia, a country in Africa. And that's where my grandmother grew up. She probably would have gone back to the mission field as well if she hadn't met my grandfather when she did and started a family with him."

"A family of missionaries," Jade smiled, beaming at him. "And you."

"What about me?" he'd asked, thinking that he didn't fit in at all with the rest of his godly family.

"You're a missionary of your own kind," she said. "Coming here to the US like you did. And even now, helping me out by making these calls… well, God could be using you in all of these moments to reach someone for Christ, you know? Look at all of these people God is bringing to you because of this, all of these people you could share His love with."

Oh, he knew what she meant. But he doubted that this could be true.

Still, though, it was on his mind long after they'd said their goodbyes that morning and then in the next few days as he'd text her to let her know he was still waiting on a call back, as their texts would turn into whole conversations, as he'd find himself for the first time in a long time smiling down at his phone each time it buzzed, always happy to hear from Jade.

She was an unexpected bit of sunshine in his life.

That's why he was smiling on Sunday morning when his phone buzzed another text at him, expecting that it was her again, laying his yueqin down so that he could reach across the table where his coffee sat among some music he was working on writing.

But it wasn't Jade's name that flashed across his phone. It was a text from a number he didn't recognize.

A text in Chinese.

"Hold up," he muttered to himself, checking his call log, matching the last number he'd called on that morning with Jade to the text.

Success. It wasn't a returned call, but as he went back to the text, he found that it was better.

Yes, I worked at House of Hope but not during that time. You might find your questions answered by a Mr. Stanley Cheng, who currently resides in New York. His number is —

Taylor copied it into his contacts immediately, sending a response back to the texter, thanking him.

New York. This would make timing a call that much easier. He had the thought as he looked outside, noting that the sun was completely up now. He could make the call right this minute.

But Jade… she'd want to be in on this call, too.

He didn't stop and think through the exact hour as he went ahead and texted her.

Have a new contact about House of Hope. Meet me in an hour, and we'll call him together?

He could see that Jade got his text immediately, and soon, she was texting back. He took his coffee to the sink as he waited on her answer, calculating how fast he could jump in the shower then get to her, thinking through a place where they could meet up —

What?! I'm freaking out over here!

So American. He couldn't keep from smiling as he read it.

But I've got church. I'm just about to start teaching Sunday school, actually.

Oh. He hadn't thought through that. Maybe he could meet her after church —

Aren't you going to church?

Uhh…no.

He considered texting her that but hesitated. He didn't want her thinking badly of him, didn't want to tell her that he hadn't been to church in forever.

Why did he care what she thought? And if it was so awful that he was out of church, why had he never felt so much conviction about it until now?

Well, that was a laugh. He'd felt conviction about it for years –

His phone buzzed with another text from Jade.

Wait – are you even a Christian? You didn't answer me the last time I asked you about it.

This girl. She was asking him questions no one had asked him since he'd come back to the States. Her boldness wasn't off putting – just surprising. And it made him want to be honest with her –

Ugh, none of my business, Taylor. But you should come to my church if you don't have one to go to this morning. I'd love to see you there.

He froze in place, considering this for a long moment. He wouldn't have to answer her question directly if he did go. Of course, he wanted to answer her question now. The thought surprised him, but it was there all the same.

He sent off a text to her before he could spend any time doubting it.

Sounds good. And we can call this guy afterwards?

There. He was going to church.

He was going to church.

Jade sent him a smiley face in response.

An hour later, Taylor was in church, sitting beside Jade.

It had been easy enough to find the place. It wasn't even that far from campus. If life had gone differently when Taylor came back to the States three years ago, this church might have been one that he would have ended up attending. He might have met Jade earlier, might have found a hint of home from the start in her friendship. Not just because she was Chinese, but because she was –

"Here," she whispered, propping half of her Bible in his lap so he could follow along with the sermon. "Since you forgot yours."

Because she was a friend. He felt that confirmed as she smiled at him, no judgment in her gaze as she turned to the passage, as her father began to preach to his congregation.

His very white congregation, Taylor noted as he looked around. Wow. Had Jade felt like a sore thumb her entire life? Had she felt as conspicuous here in small town USA as he had in the heart of China?

Taylor could feel his mind wandering as he thought through it, as he wondered at what it must have been like for her to grow up in this established church, as his mind went back to his very Chinese church back in Shanghai. An underground church, more like a small group when they'd started meeting with just a few new believers. A group that had grown more and more, that was always under the government's eye. His pastor had been arrested more than once for his faith, had found his times in prison to be great times of instruction in the word of God from other pastors similarly imprisoned, and had shared boldly even with those who had thrown him into prison in the first place.

Pastor Zhao was passionate about his faith.

Not unlike this pastor, Jade's father, Taylor noted as the older man continued preaching from the book of Romans.

"But where sin increased, grace abounded all the more," Mark Matthews read in a bold, unwavering voice. "When we read this in context, we realize what a helpless situation we find ourselves in. And what should we always do?"

"Read the Bible in context," Jade repeated along with everyone else in the building.

Except for Taylor, of course, who just looked around in surprise before glancing back at Jade.

She just smiled at him.

"So we read it in context," Mark continued, smiling. "And we see that because of Adam's sin, we were all born into disobedience. Friends, you can't save yourselves because you're born bad. People are not inherently good. They – we – are inherently evil. It's who we are. And if you doubt that, we'll be happy to let you serve in the church nursery, working with two year olds."

There was some laughter at this, and Taylor found himself smiling as well.

"We're all born with a sinful heart," Mark had continued on. "And because of that, we're helpless. Millions and billions of us, born under the curse, helpless to save ourselves. That's the kind of context we have to keep in mind as we approach Paul's next words about Christ, about the second Adam. Jesus is a picture of Adam, and he turns the paradigm on its head. By Adam's disobedience, we are condemned."

Here, he smiled at the congregation.

"But by Jesus's righteousness, we are saved."

Taylor knew this. He'd heard it all of his life, in Mandarin and English both, over and over again…

"We aren't saved by works," Mark kept on. "As if we could do good on our own, since we're inherently evil. Like I might have already said. Our sinful nature and the ensuing condemnation due to us because of it is Adam's gift to us. But Christ's gift to us breaks the curse! His righteousness, His obedience on the cross, His sinless life given for you and me – that blood, that righteousness, that sacrifice – saves us. And it's not a once and done deal. Sin reigned in us because of Adam, but because of Christ, grace can reign in us. And grace reigning in us means that every day we have grace, every moment we have grace, every living breathing second of our lives, we have grace."

There were several amens at this.

Taylor knew all of this. He'd heard it before.

But something about it tugged at him.

Had it been that long since he'd heard the word of God? It had been a while, he had to admit to himself. Maybe once in a while, he would pick up his Bible, dust it off, and spend a little bit of time in it. But not long. He'd just feel convicted when he read, the words reminding him of who he had been and how far he'd fallen.

But these words…

It was like a whisper, a familiar voice that didn't dim out and die away. A voice that only got louder and louder the longer he considered what Mark was saying.

"And then," Mark said with a heavy sigh, "that leads right to the next question that I'm sure many of you are asking yourselves. It's what Paul says next, because he knew where your mind would go as well. 'What shall we say then? Are we to continue in sin that grace may abound?' And I won't get into the answer this week since that's next week's sermon… but you can go ahead and peek at the answer before we get there together."

Taylor found himself smiling at this, at the comfortable feeling in this church, at the way that there was joy in the word of God, not just from the pastor but from the congregation as many smiled over their Bibles, looking ahead to see what God would say next.

Like Jade as she studied it beside Taylor, nudging him in the side.

"He always tells us to look ahead," she whispered. "He can't keep surprises."

Taylor smiled at this as well, liking the exuberance of the pastor as he continued with an invitation, calling each of them to consider where they were and who they were in Christ.

Taylor bowed his head along with everyone else, feeling that whisper from God again in his heart, wondering over the words of grace.

He was still thinking about it as the church dismissed, as several people came over to meet him, and as this community of faith very nearly surrounded him.

He should have felt panicked or strange about it, given his distance from God. But there was something familiar about this, about being with a body of believers, something warm that reminded him of home. Nothing but white faces all around, but the spirit here was the same as it had been back home in China.

Acceptance. Kindness. Grace.

So much so that when the church was nearly empty and Jade introduced him to her father, he began by saying thank you.

"For what?" Mark asked, his hand in Taylor's, a smile on his face.

"For the sermon," he said. "Those words… they were good."

Mark didn't know just how good and just how much they'd gotten Taylor thinking.

"Those weren't my words," Mark said warmly. "Just the words of God. And I'm glad you were here. Jade's told us so much about you and all the ways you've been helping her –"

"Hello, there!"

And there was a woman about Taylor's mother's age, coming right up to him and reaching out for his hand, holding it in her own as he gave it to her.

"I'm Molly Matthews," she said, smiling. "It's so good to meet you!"

Warm and inviting. Kind and sweet. So familiar.

Taylor glanced at Jade, an amused smile on his lips. For a mother and daughter who were in no way biologically connected, they bore a striking resemblance to one another in spirit.

Jade grinned back at him. "Mom, this is Taylor."

"Oh!" Molly exclaimed, dropping his hand and hugging him close now, no inhibitions left as she released him a few seconds later and held his face in her hands, tears in her eyes. "Jade's Chinese friend! You've been God's gift to us, Taylor!"

Wow. What a welcome.

"Molly," Mark said, laughing.

"I'm sorry," Molly said, wiping at her eyes as she'd begun crying now. "I get emotional, Taylor. But with all that you're doing for Jade, can you blame me?"

Yes, well, that was why he was here. All this talk about him being God's gift to anyone (highly unlikely) had him forcing his mind back to what he was here to do. He and Jade were going to call this new contact and –

"Come and have lunch at our house," Molly said, his hands in hers again. "We want to know all about you!"

Again, this was a moment where someone else might have been freaked out. It was a lot to handle all at once, coming back to church, meeting the pastor and his wife, and grappling with the issue of grace. And Taylor, who had felt nothing but guilt and shame when it came to the things of God for so long now, should have been more hesitant than anyone to go to a pastor's home.

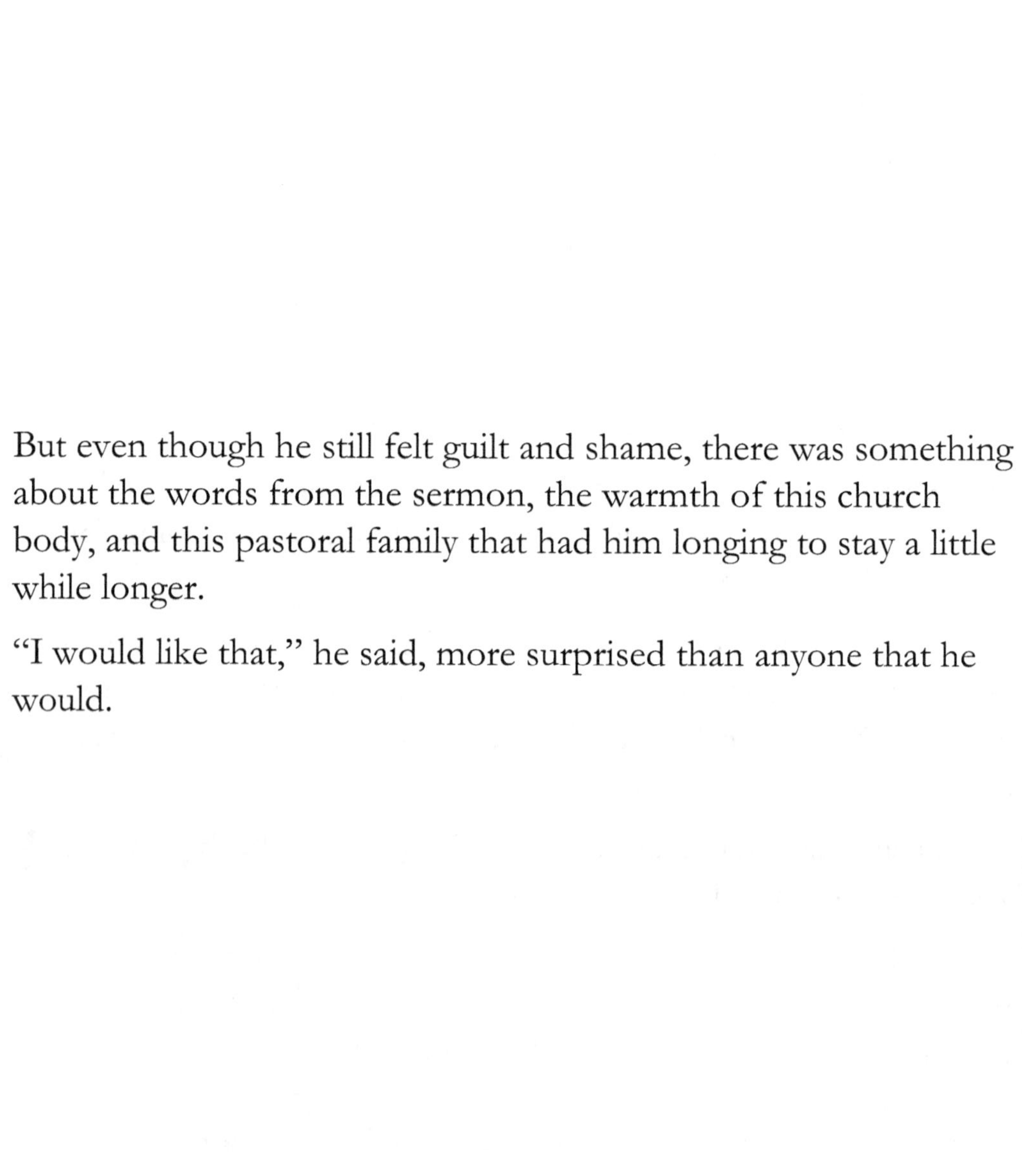

But even though he still felt guilt and shame, there was something about the words from the sermon, the warmth of this church body, and this pastoral family that had him longing to stay a little while longer.

"I would like that," he said, more surprised than anyone that he would.

~Jade~

Taylor Robinson was in her house.

Jade smiled at the oddity of this, of how even though it was unexpected it felt right, having him here at the dinner table, eating lunch with them like they did every Sunday, fitting right in as though he'd always been a part of them.

She'd expected her parents to pepper him with endless questions about China, about the search he was helping Jade with, and about this newest development. That last one was certainly on Jade's mind as she anxiously waited for Taylor to get on his phone, call that new contact, and have another conversation on her behalf.

But Mark and Molly seemed more determined to get to know Taylor for who he was and not for what he was doing for Jade and, by association, for them.

Maybe Jade should take a page or two from their books.

"Music education," Molly said, enthusiasm in her voice. "Taylor, I was a teacher for years and years. Back before we adopted Jade. Would have kept at it past retirement eligibility likely had we not decided that I should stay home with Jade because of some of her needs early on."

"And she would likely have jumped right back into teaching," Jade put in helpfully, "once I was older. Which she did, in a roundabout way."

"Molly runs our church's preschool program," Mark said. "Which is teaching —"

"But not elementary school," Molly put in helpfully, grinning over at Taylor. "And not public school. It's very different. And Taylor knows all about it with the education classes he's taking."

"Music education is different," he said as he continued to eat, smiling over at Jade's mother warmly. "But essentially… yes. It's the same in a lot of ways."

"What are your plans?" Mark asked. "After graduation, I mean. Jade tells us that you don't play the typical band instruments, which is what I'm guessing music education amounts to at the secondary level, at least in a small school context."

Taylor glanced over at Jade, and she smiled back at him. Surely it was okay that she'd told her parents so much about him. It probably made her look like she spent all of her time thinking about him, talking about him –

Well, she did spend a lot of time thinking about him, even if she kept most of those thoughts to herself. She felt her mind going that way again as he continued chatting with her parents, so friendly and so personable.

The love you and leave you kind.

Crenshaw's words came back to her, but she pushed the thought away. That's not who this guy was –

"You're right," he said to her dad. "My dad is a music teacher at the secondary level, but his forte is and has always been traditional band instruments, whereas mine is something completely different."

"Strings," Molly said. "That's what Jade tells us. And not orchestra strings. Country music!"

Jade cringed a little. How had her mother gotten this from her description of bluegrass instruments?

"That," Taylor smiled broadly. "And Chinese instruments, some of which are played most commonly in the more rural parts of China so… Chinese country music as well."

He looked over at Jade, and she could tell he was holding in a laugh.

"I bet that sounds weird," she said, unable to keep from laughing.

He joined her. "Maybe a little."

"Do they teach Chinese country music in schools now?" Molly asked, completely serious, even as the question made Jade giggle even more.

"They don't, regrettably," Taylor said with a sigh. "Which is part of what I'm struggling with when it comes to post-graduation plans. I'll be equipped to teach band, to do music lessons, even to teach the basics of music at the elementary level."

"But…" Mark said, hearing the unspoken words in Taylor's voice.

"But I'm not sure that I want to do any of those things," he said.

Jade was surprised by this, not only by the admission but by the fact that he was sharing this with her parents after only just meeting them.

But her parents were like that. There was something about them that encouraged others to be completely open and honest. They were good listeners, encouragers and empathizers. Jade had certainly reaped the benefit of all of those qualities over the years, and as she grew older, she prayed that God would bring out the same characteristics in her.

Maybe He was, as Taylor looked over at her again.

"It's been challenging getting to know Jade, seeing her love for music and the way that she embraces it not as a means to an end – to a job, to financial security, to a career – but as what it was meant to be. Something for enjoyment. An art to be savored, not to be tweaked into a paycheck."

"Hmm," Mark murmured. "And I guess that gets lost in your classes, in all the work you've done towards getting your degree?"

"It does," Taylor said honestly. "Maybe if I had majored in music alone, if I had my sights set on a career in performance, it would be different. But I chose a different route when I started, thinking that I needed some future job security. And I just assumed that education – that teaching – was something anyone could do and not a calling, like it is for my dad."

Molly nodded at this. "A calling. I like that."

"What do you think your calling is?" Mark asked him.

The way he asked such a personal question wasn't done in a pushy way. Just in a fatherly, kind way. Jade could see that Taylor took it just the way it was intended.

"I'm not sure," he said. "A long time ago, I thought my music and my skills might be used by God in some way, but I don't know now. Or even if…"

Jade could see the struggle in his eyes. Mark and Molly could as well, given their words.

"God can use it all," Mark said. "And not just your music, not just your talents. But everything that makes you who you are. Your experiences – good and bad – can all be used for His good. And for yours."

Amen. Wasn't that Jade's own story? How God used all the sad parts of her story, of her limitations, of her questions, for His good and hers as well?

"I'd like to believe that," Taylor said softly, regret in his tone.

Jade wondered at that, too.

The love you and leave you kind.

"But graduation looms ahead," Taylor shrugged, "and I've got to find some way to pay the bills. So teaching…"

"It doesn't mean forever," Molly said, smiling. "Maybe God will use teaching to provide for you in just this next season, and maybe the time He spends doing so will prepare you for whatever He has next."

Taylor smiled a little at this. "That's a good thought."

"I can't imagine that God doesn't have His eyes and His hands on you, Taylor," Mark said confidently. "Especially not when He's placed you in just the right place at the right time for Jade."

Amen. Jade believed that as well and was so thankful that He'd done just that.

"Maybe God has put you into Jade's life at just the right moment because of who you are, where you've been," Mark said, smiling. "And maybe God has even more planned here than we can imagine right now."

~Taylor~

At just the right place at the right time for Jade.

It had been so easy to relax with the Matthews family, with Jade's parents, as they'd given him good counsel and so much encouragement, that he'd very nearly forgotten the whole reason he'd come to the church and then to their house in the first place.

Mark's words brought him back, though. And before too long, they were all gathered around him at the table, waiting to make the call. Molly had even brought out a file folder of Jade's documents, so as to be prepared for any questions, and Taylor noted with some confusion that only one of them was in Chinese.

Did Jade not have any other documentation?

He pushed the thought aside as he dialed the number and greeted the man who answered in Mandarin, holding back a smile as Molly raised her eyebrows and grinned at Jade in delight, with Mark smiling as well.

They were just like Jade. So positive and encouraging –

"Hi, yes, this is Stanley Cheng."

Taylor blinked at this. Mr. Cheng wasn't just a fluent English speaker. He was an American, judging by that accent.

"Hello, Mr. Cheng," Taylor said, switching to English, thankful that the Matthews family would be able to understand everything easily now. "My name is Taylor Robinson, and I got your number from a colleague of yours. At House of Hope in Shanghai?"

He posed it as a question, half expecting that this would be another dead end.

"Yes," Mr. Cheng said, his tone more upbeat now. "I worked at House of Hope."

He could see the joy in Jade's eyes at this… and the hesitation, the fear that they'd be let down again.

Taylor had the same fear, even as he swallowed and gave Mr. Cheng the specific dates.

"Oh, well, I wasn't there during those dates," he said.

Taylor refrained from dropping his head right onto the table.

"May I ask why you're curious about that specific time frame?" Mr. Cheng asked.

And so Taylor told him about Jade, about her adoption, and about her search for her birth mother.

Mr. Cheng said nothing for a long moment.

"What do you know about House of Hope, Mr. Robinson?" he finally asked.

The question caught Taylor off guard, but he quickly recovered.

"I know that it was for children with medical issues," he said. "Children from Shanghai."

But even as he said it, he looked back at Jade and wondered… well, he wondered if that was all that House of Hope did.

"It was more than that," Mr. Cheng said. "And I assume that you want to know the details of your friend's particular adoption so that she might be able to trace her roots, so to speak. And that she intends to start in Shanghai?"

"That's all we've got," Taylor said, looking over at Molly's documentation. "And I mean that literally. We've only got her documentation from China, which says Shanghai."

"But was she born in Shanghai?" Mr. Cheng asked.

This was the question. Because if she wasn't (which Taylor suspected the more he thought about it), then they weren't even looking in the right place.

Jade looked to her mother expectantly.

Molly smiled. "Oh, yes, she was born in Shanghai," she said, her voice raised so that it could be heard over Taylor's phone.

Then that was that.

Right?

"Mr. Cheng, did you get that?" Taylor asked, glancing over at Jade with an encouraging smile.

"I did," Mr. Cheng answered. "But are they certain of that?"

Taylor looked at Jade in question. Jade shrugged, turning to her parents. "Why would…?"

"That's what this says," Molly said, handing one of the documents over to Taylor. "Right?"

Yes, it was.

"She was born in Shanghai far as we know," Mark said now, looking at Taylor's phone, concern in his eyes. "Are you saying that there's a chance that… well, that she wasn't?"

"I'm saying that House of Hope didn't just exist for the children of Shanghai," Mr. Cheng said. "We brought in children from all parts of the country."

But that begged another question.

"Well, wouldn't they document that?" Taylor asked. "Wouldn't Jade's birth certificate state something other than Shanghai if she was one of those children?"

Mr. Cheng hesitated for a long moment.

"It's complicated," he finally said.

No kidding. Taylor had no idea what any of this meant, and neither did the Matthews family, judging by the way they were watching one another.

"Are you saying that Jade wasn't born in Shanghai?" Mark asked.

"I can't say definitively since I wasn't there at the time," Mr. Cheng answered. "But there's a good chance."

Taylor's eyes trailed over Jade's face for the thousandth time. But this was a more discerning journey as he took in her features, compared them to what he knew, and considered it all.

"Molly," he said to Jade's mother, "did you ever ask about Jade's background? When you were in Shanghai?"

"No," she said, looking distraught at the thought of what they might have missed. "We didn't focus on that. We only wanted to look forward to the future. So when they gave us documentation that she was born in Shanghai…"

They'd not questioned it. They'd not known to question it.

But Taylor did. So did Mr. Cheng.

"I suggest," the latter said thoughtfully, "that you do some more digging and consider the possibility that Shanghai isn't where you need to be looking after all."

~Jade~

The week that followed that Sunday had been a hard one. The conversation with Mr. Cheng had ended with more questions than answers, and while he'd told Taylor that he'd make some calls around and see what he could find, he hadn't left Jade with much hope.

They'd had so little to go on at the beginning. Born in Shanghai, adopted from House of Hope. And now, they had even less, with half of what they'd known up in the air, a mystery to be solved.

There were one and a half billion people in China. Even knowing where to look still made for impossible odds when it came to finding one individual without any other information. And now that they didn't know where to look?

Hopeless.

She'd seen Taylor a few times during the week, even grabbed lunch with him in between classes a couple of times, and he'd had no new news. But he'd told her to not give up quite yet, then had done a great job of distracting her with talk of other things, with stories about the concert he was gearing up for with his ensemble, the work he needed to get done to be prepared for his own senior recital, and the never-ending mishaps associated with the language lab and its archaic software.

She'd found herself laughing with him, appreciating that he was able to make her forget it all for just a little while.

Her mother was doing her best to make her forget it, too.

"I'm glad we took this girls' day," she told Jade that next weekend as they sat side by side in their chairs at the salon. "And I can't for the life of me figure out why we didn't do this sooner."

"We have done this," Jade said. "Visits to the nail salon, shopping trips, coffee dates – it's like our M.O., Mom."

It always had been, even when Jade was little, when Molly would get her all set up in the recliner at the pedicure place, taking her braces off her legs as she chattered on and on about how she couldn't decide on a tea party at the little tea room in town or a milkshake at the drive-thru, leaving the choice up to Jade. They'd always spend the rest of their day wiggling their new toes and laughing over snacks, mother and daughter bonding at its finest.

There were more serious days, too, where Jade would talk through some of the more difficult parts of those preteen days, then the adolescent years with her mother, with Molly listening supportively, offering advice when it was needed and sometimes when it wasn't. Neither one of them got it right all the time, this mother daughter relationship, but they were always trying, praying together, with Molly teaching Jade what scripture said, how God called them both to live, and letting her know at every turn in the road that Jesus loved her.

This trip wasn't so different from all the others.

"No, this is totally different," Molly insisted, reaching across to pat Jade's hand. "Because we've never done this! Virgin hair – isn't that what she said?" Her mother gestured dramatically to the foil on her head.

Jade couldn't help but smile at this. "Virgin hair, yes. Untouched by chemicals."

"Not anymore," Molly said, wiggling her eyebrows. "I'm going to be a blonde."

"It's going to take more than one trip for you to become a blonde," Jade countered. "You heard her tell you that."

"And she said it would take you several, *several* trips to become a blonde," Molly laughed.

"If that," Jade laughed, too. "I half expect my Chinese heritage to come out swinging and fighting against lightening my hair even a little."

"Well, I'm glad for that," Molly sighed. "You're the most beautiful brunette I've ever known. Highlights are one thing, but changing your hair more drastically than that would be a crime against who you are."

Who you are.

Jade's mind went back to that talk with Mr. Cheng, to China, to all of the unanswered questions…

"Your dad told me that Taylor came to Wednesday night Bible study," Molly said.

"Yeah," Jade affirmed, thinking about how surprised she'd been when he'd asked her about it. "He told me he was interested in coming back to the church when we had lunch together on Tuesday."

Her mother watched her for a long moment.

"What?" Jade asked, feeling her scrutiny.

"You're spending a lot of time together, you and Taylor," Molly said.

"Well, he's helping me with everything," Jade said, though most of their conversations lately hadn't been about that at all. No, they'd been about her classes, about some mutual friends they had in the music department now, about some of the campus events they were both planning on going to, and about – surprise to Jade – the church.

She didn't know where Taylor was spiritually speaking, and she was surprised to find that while she was usually bold about asking these questions – had even been bold with him when they first met – that she was hesitant to speak so boldly now.

Something was going on with him. God was doing something in his life. And Jade wanted to step back, to let God do His work, to trust Him with that.

"And he's really enjoying going through the book of Romans," Jade said, remembering how Taylor had asked about the details on what her dad preached on Wednesdays, seemingly glad when he heard that Mark did a review and a more in-depth look at Sunday's text on Wednesday nights.

"He's a good guy," Molly said. "Maybe in a transitional place in his life, career wise and…"

And she didn't finish the thought, but Jade heard it anyway. She'd been thinking the same thing.

Spiritually.

He was a believer, that much was clear. He'd said as much to Jade as he'd told her about his experiences in the Chinese church he'd grown up in while in the US, then his home church in China.

"I put my trust in Christ while sitting under Pastor Li in Houston. I was ten," he'd told her as he'd walked her across campus to the chemistry building, to her next class, keeping her pace and not even appearing to be bothered by it. "But I made another decision when I was fifteen, when I was being discipled by Pastor Zhao in Shanghai."

"And what decision was that?" she asked.

"To be a missionary," he said.

At this, she'd stared at him, nearly stopping on the sidewalk.

"Not vocationally," he'd said, scratching the back of his neck. "But with my life. With all my life, no matter where God sent me, no matter what He purposed for me to do."

"I love that," Jade had answered back, truly loving everything about that.

"But then, I came here," Taylor had said.

And then, he hadn't said anything else. Jade had wanted to ask him about it, but they'd been at her building by then.

And the look on his face had her remembering other words.

The love you and leave you kind.

What had gone on during Taylor's first year of college? And why had it so changed him?

She wasn't sure. But Taylor was definitely in a season of searching, of transition, of – Jade prayed – finding his way back to Christ.

"And he's cute," Molly added, forcing Jade back to the hair salon, to the cacophony of hair dryers, chatter and laughter, and music playing all around them.

Jade blinked at her reflection, at the foil wrapped in her hair, at the blush that rose on her cheeks at this.

"Umm… maybe," she managed.

"Maybe nothing," Molly said. "He's cute. And definitely interested in you."

It wasn't like Jade had never had a boyfriend. She'd had a couple of them in high school, boys from the band who were also in her honors classes, boys who were active in their own churches. She'd gone on plenty of dates, had felt that rush of young infatuation a time or two, and was no stranger to romantic feelings.

But this was different. Taylor wasn't in any kind of place spiritually speaking that she wanted to go. And apart from him helping her with her search and being a friend to her, there was nothing more on his end… right?

And there was nothing more on her end. Except that, yes, she could agree that he was cute.

"He's interested in this great mystery I'm living," Jade said. "Who is Jade Matthews? It's like a neverending circle of questions, over and over again."

That was the truth. The hard, sad truth.

"I know who Jade Matthews is," Molly said. "She's a brilliant student, an incredible friend, a great musician, a loving Sunday school teacher, the best daughter in the entire world –"

And Molly choked up at that last one.

Jade looked over at her, ready to apologize for saying anything at all. Her mom had always been emotional like this, but this conversation – this whole ordeal – had made her even more so.

"I'm sorry that this is hard for you," she said softly. "That was never my intention when I started looking for my birth mother."

"I know that," Molly said, fighting with the cape she wore so that she could wipe at her eyes with her fingers. "And it's not hard, Jade. Not in the way that you think. I'm not sitting here feeling insecure about us, about what I have with you. I'm just sad, knowing that all of this is not easy for you. I just want easy answers for you. Good answers. All that you ever wanted."

Jade nodded, appreciating this.

"And besides," Molly said, "you didn't let me finish."

"Finish what?"

"Telling you the most important part of who Jade Matthews is."

"And what's that?" Jade asked.

"Jade Matthews," Molly said, "is loved and treasured by God."

That was the most important part.

And as the day went from hair appointments to makeovers, from shopping to coffee, she kept this promise in her heart, even as her mother hugged her goodbye and dropped her back off at the dorm.

Loved and treasured by God.

That was enough. It always would be, no matter what she found out.

Taylor was going to get some answers.

He was even more determined after seeing the crestfallen look on Jade's face after that call from Mr. Cheng after church on Sunday. He'd seen her since then, and she'd been her upbeat, cheerful self. But still, Taylor could tell when he'd mention China and the way they were waiting to hear back from any other contacts that it was still weighing heavy on her mind and her heart.

He resolved that he wasn't going to put her through more of these hard conversations until he had real answers. Maybe that was wrong, continuing on with his search in secret, doing this without her knowing, but he couldn't bear the thought of hurting her worse when any of the leads he was pursuing turned out to be more dead ends.

Jade was special to him now. And while he couldn't sort out all of the reasons behind how he felt about her and what it might all mean, he knew that protecting her heart was a priority now.

He reminded himself of that when the call came in on Saturday night.

"Is this Taylor Robinson?"

It was a woman's voice – an American woman's voice – that came over the line. Taylor's heart fell just a little. This wasn't another Chinese individual who could direct him to more information about Jade. This call was probably about student teaching in the spring, one of any number of calls he'd been getting about potential opportunities.

He'd taken Mark's words to heart after church on Sunday. Teaching right now for a season didn't mean that it was for life. And while he did wonder at the idea that God would use it to prepare him for something else down the line, he found himself coming to peace with the reality that would be his shortly – finding a job and still trying to keep the love he had for music as he did so.

Maybe the summer and that band camp experience had just soured him. And what was more, maybe a lot of his angst when it came to music education was more about how differently his life had gone when he'd arrived in the US. Was it possible that his feelings about his life and his choices only seemed magnified in the music department where it had all started, making him dread the very career path that he'd once anticipated?

Taylor wasn't sure. He enjoyed the bluegrass section that he taught, more and more every day. And he found himself even enjoying the music department again these days, especially on those occasions when he would run into Jade, coming and going from her woodwind ensemble.

All that said, he'd started looking back into student teaching opportunities. And that's probably what this phone call was about.

He shifted his mind that direction. A future job was a good thing, but even with his recent change of heart, it still wasn't nearly as exciting as helping Jade.

"Yes," he said, injecting enthusiasm in his voice despite this let down. "This is Taylor."

"Taylor," the woman said. "My name is Laura Hemsworth. I got a call from Stanley Cheng, telling me that I just might be the right person to answer your questions about House of Hope."

And with that, Taylor was once again hopeful, enthusiastic.

"Really?" he said. "But you're an American."

Stanley Cheng had been as well, of course, but this woman didn't have a Chinese surname.

Laura laughed a little at this. "Yes, I'm an American," she said. "And I was an American eighteen years ago when I was living in Shanghai and working at House of Hope as an English translator."

Eighteen years ago.

"Eighteen years ago," Taylor said. "That's exactly when my friend was there."

"So Stanley told me."

Answers. He was going to get answers.

"What do you know about House of Hope, Taylor?" she asked carefully.

Taylor understood the hesitation in her tone, remembered that Mr. Cheng had asked the same question.

"I understand that House of Hope took in babies from other parts of the country," he said, on his feet now, pacing his small apartment. "I already knew that House of Hope was for special needs children, but it wasn't until I spoke with Mr. Cheng that I learned it wasn't just for children from Shanghai but from the whole of China."

"That's right," Laura said. "House of Hope was funded by an American organization, and what we did wasn't illegal – not in the slightest – but the Chinese government took a… well, I'm not sure how to say it."

Oh, but Taylor did. His parents were in China legally, of course, but the government took a heightened interest in everything they did.

Mark's words about Taylor coming along at the right moment for Jade, with who he was and where he'd been, came to mind.

He got what Laura Hemsworth was saying.

"They took a great interest in what you were doing," Taylor finished for her.

"Aptly said," Laura agreed with a sigh. "And our interest in ethnic minority groups in China was something that the government was very suspicious of, as I'm sure you can understand."

Ethnic minority groups.

Jade's face flashed through Taylor's mind, the way her eyes were just slightly different than most of the girls he'd known in China, her smile, the color of her skin…

This. Taylor took a breath, his mind working quickly now.

"The government is very careful with its fringe populations," Laura continued on, unaware of the leaps and bounds his mind was taking. "And they tend to view any work with even these groups' most vulnerable members as suspect. If the government had its way, the children – even the handicapped children – from these groups wouldn't leave the very small pockets of China where they live and are, for lack of a better word, contentedly kept to themselves."

Taylor thought about Jade, her face in his mind. Chinese, yes. But even from that first day, there had been something about her that was different…

"Ethnic minority groups," he murmured, thinking through it.

"Glorious people groups," Laura breathed. "With their own traditions and histories that remain, in some areas, untouched by mainstream Chinese culture, you see. Groups that we were not to work directly with as House of Hope. When we got calls from other parts of China, regarding children in need, we went and got those babies, brought them to Shanghai, and found them families. And we listed their home provinces on their birth information in most cases." She paused for a long moment. "Except when those children were from specific groups. Then, we sometimes listed them as Shanghai born on official documents."

Oh, Jade. If this was true for her, where would they even begin to look for her birth mother?

Taylor ran his hands through his hair.

"I'm not saying that this is the case for your friend," Laura said.

"For Jade," Taylor supplied.

"Yes, Jade," she repeated. "But it's a possibility. A very good possibility given the number of times we did things like this, sending nannies – for lack of a better word – out to the different provinces, having them get the babies, and having them travel back to Shanghai with them as though they were Han children, children like the majority of people in China. And once these children from these outlying groups got to Shanghai, any official documentation on them lacked any details apart from Shanghai. That's where we rewrote their history, so to speak, making it as though their lives didn't begin until they got to us."

Taylor wasn't sure how to feel about this. It felt deceptive, but what would the alternative have been?

He wasn't sure, but he suspected that Jade would have never left China, never left that orphanage, never gotten the help she needed…

"What were the dates you were looking at again?" Laura asked him. "From her first day at House of Hope until her adoption?"

"Does it matter?" he asked bleakly, taking Laura at her word, at what she'd just explained, knowing that there would be no official documentation.

"It does," she said, her voice lowered. "Because we may have lacked official documentation, but I kept records of each and every child I worked with while I was there. And I have those records with me now."

Taylor swallowed nervously, hardly able to believe this.

"Taylor?" she prompted.

"Yes," he said with a breathless laugh, then he gave the dates to her, readying himself to hear that she had no record of that particular child, that she had no answers –

"I was there when she arrived," Laura said, a smile in the words. "And I remember her."

No way.

"Oh," Taylor barely managed.

"She had cerebral palsy, right?" she said. "A darling little thing. Only a couple of months old."

Yes. Taylor could hardly believe it.

"Yes, that's exactly right," he said.

"Well, that was a special case," she said, and he could almost hear the smile in her voice. "Not just because that baby girl had very special needs, but because by the time she came to us, she'd traveled farther than any baby at House of Hope ever had. Not that it would have been listed in her information, though, nor would her adoptive parents have ever known."

No, they hadn't.

"How is she?" Laura asked. "How is Jade?"

And now, she was talking about Jade as though she'd known her. And she had. She'd known her from those first days at House of Hope.

Taylor couldn't keep from smiling. "She's amazing," he said, thinking of Jade. "So smart. Funny. Sweet and kind. And godly. Beautiful…"

All of this. But he found himself surprised by the level of emotion in his voice as he relayed the information.

"She's a freshman in college," he said, clearing his throat. "Pre-pharmacy major. Plays the flute for fun. And teaches Sunday school to preschoolers at her dad's church."

"And the cerebral palsy?" Laura asked.

He'd nearly forgotten all about it in talking through all that Jade was.

"She copes well," he said. "Lots of surgery and therapy when she was little. And even more determination and perseverance now that she's an adult, living her life as normally as possible."

"Nothing sounds normal about the young woman you described," Laura said, clear emotion in her voice. "She sounds very special."

She was. So very special.

"She is," he managed, emotional just thinking about her.

"Would you like to hear more about where she came from?" Laura asked. "And how she ended up at House of Hope?"

Yes. Yes, he would.

"Yes, please," he said, readying himself for the truth.

He got off the phone with Laura Hemsworth an hour later and let out a loud, exhausted breath.

All of that information. All of that hard information.

But it was good. It was so good because he finally had answers for Jade.

This didn't call for a text or even a phone chat. No, he needed to see her face to face for this conversation. And it was going to be a long one. A hard one, too, but not one without some celebration.

That's what it called for. Celebration.

A plan formed in his mind, and he sent her a text even as he paced his apartment.

You free tonight?

He began straightening up as he waited for her to return his text, moving stacks of music, taking dirty dishes to the sink, and marveling over what a slob he could be in his own space.

He didn't think about it much most of the time because he didn't have people over. But if Jade was going to be here –

Yeah… why?

He answered her text back quickly.

I'm going to be by to pick you up in about ten minutes.

If that text was presumptive or bossy either one, Jade didn't comment on it. And after he'd called and placed an order at the restaurant then driven over to her dorm, he'd found her waiting there for him.

She looked… different somehow.

"I like your hair," he said as she'd gotten into his car, wondering if it was just her hair that was different. It was lighter in places, not its normal dark black.

How had she done that?

And her face… she'd done something different there, too. And wow, all of it combined took Jade, who was already beautiful, and made her…

Well. Made her even more beautiful. He wouldn't have thought that was possible, but there had been the proof, sitting in his passenger seat.

She'd smiled at him as she'd clicked her seatbelt in place.

"Thank you, Taylor," she said even as he put the car in reverse and headed out.

And she didn't ask any questions. Not about what they were doing or about whether or not he'd heard anything more in the search for her birth records or her mother either way. No, Jade had just asked him about how his day had gone, if he'd gotten any of the work done that he'd told her about earlier, chatting with him easily about his music, and agreeing with him that searching for student teaching positions still made good sense.

She was like that – thoughtful and kind. Taylor found himself asking her the same questions as he drove to the Chinese restaurant, smiling at her answers, befuddled by the way she trusted him enough to just jump in his car with him and head out, not even wondering where they were going or what they were doing.

Until he jumped out at the restaurant, telling her he'd only be a few minutes, and came back with a couple of bags filled with containers.

"Uhh, what's all this?" Jade asked as he passed the bags over to her and got back in the driver's seat.

"Dinner," he said. "I wanted to talk with you, but I thought we could do it over dinner."

She looked at the containers, a perplexed expression on her face.

"What is this?" she asked.

"Chinese food," he said, as he began to drive back to his apartment. "Except not quite, because this place is owned and run by white people."

Seriously, how was this town so white?

"Oh," Jade said very simply.

"What?" he asked, glancing back over at her. "What are you thinking?"

"Well, I don't... I don't like Chinese food." She sounded almost apologetic.

"You don't like Chinese food?" he asked, disbelief in his tone. "What don't you like about it?"

She made a little face. "Well, it's just spicy. And different..."

He bit back a smile. "You don't like Chinese food."

"I know," she sighed. "I'm a picky eater, Taylor."

"You mean the perfect girl has a flaw?" he said, a laugh escaping as he did so.

The perfect girl. Yes, he'd begun to think of her like that.

"I hardly think that being a picky eater is a flaw," she laughed with him. "I have discerning taste. In music. In food. In men."

He couldn't keep from looking over at her in outright surprise at this.

She burst out laughing.

"I'm just joking, Taylor," she said. "Well, not about the men part. I don't just jump in any guy's car and go anywhere with him."

But she'd done that with him. Before he could think through the implications of this, she kept on.

"And I'm really not kidding when it comes to food either. I *am* a picky eater. That said, some of this smells really good."

"I'm glad to hear it," he said, smiling over at her.

And once he got her back to his apartment and laid it all out in front of her, she was a good sport, trying it all. There was only minimal gagging over some of it, followed by so much giggling, and when she got to the mushu pork, she smiled appreciatively at him.

"This one isn't so bad," she said. "I could stand more of it."

"Stand more of it," he said, plating up the great majority of it for her along with some of the steamed rice, putting it in front of her on the counter where she sat on one of his barstools and handing her a set of chopsticks from his stash.

"There's no way I can use these," she said.

Because of her cerebral palsy maybe? He hadn't even thought about that, about her muscle coordination, and hadn't meant to offend her –

"Because I don't know how, Taylor," she said, shaking her head at him. "Come on, man. I'm not inept. Just American."

"Okay, well, here," he said, leaning on the counter close to her, demonstrating with his own hands how to hold them, expertly using them to pick up a piece of kung pao chicken with a bit of rice and putting it right into his mouth. "Easy peasy."

"So you say," she murmured, twisting her fingers and still not getting it just right.

After watching her struggle for a few seconds, Taylor reached out and took her hand in his, moving her fingers.

"You would think you'd have more dexterity as a flute player," he muttered.

"You'd think," she agreed with another cute giggle, "but you'd be wrong."

"Jade," he laughed as her fingers refused to work the right way and as she laughed even louder. He finally put down the chopsticks altogether and put his hands over hers.

And his laughter died away at the feel of that, of the way that Jade's hand relaxed into his, the way her eyes met his.

Did she feel it, too?

"Okay," he said, clearing his throat a little, his voice subdued now, his mind warning him that he couldn't want more from her than friendship. Because he wasn't good enough for her –

"Maybe I need to just use a fork," she said. "No shame in that, huh?"

"You're breaking my heart," he managed around a laugh.

She was doing something to his heart most definitely.

He couldn't keep thinking like this. Couldn't keep letting himself feel things for her.

He had to get down to business, to what this was really about, to why she was here, to why he'd orchestrated it all just so.

And so he finally did as they were finishing up their meal.

"I heard from someone who worked at House of Hope when you were there," he said once they'd cleared away the containers and Jade was admiring all of his instruments on stands throughout the small living room.

"What?" she asked, turning to him in surprise. "Who?"

"Her name was Laura Hemsworth," he said, sitting down on the couch and gesturing for her to do the same. "Come sit with me, Jade."

This would be a hard conversation, and maybe that's why he'd been leading up to it all night.

Hard but good, he reminded himself.

"I'm not sure why you didn't tell me that as soon as you picked me up," she said, "but tell me now. Please."

Where to begin?

"Do you remember how Mr. Cheng brought up the question of where you were born?" he asked. "How he seemed to think there might be some reasonable doubt about Shanghai?"

"Yeah," she said with a sigh. "It's almost all I've been able to think about. Because if I wasn't born in Shanghai, where do I even start when it comes to finding my birth mother?"

It would be impossible without knowing where she'd been born.

But Taylor knew. And soon Jade would, too.

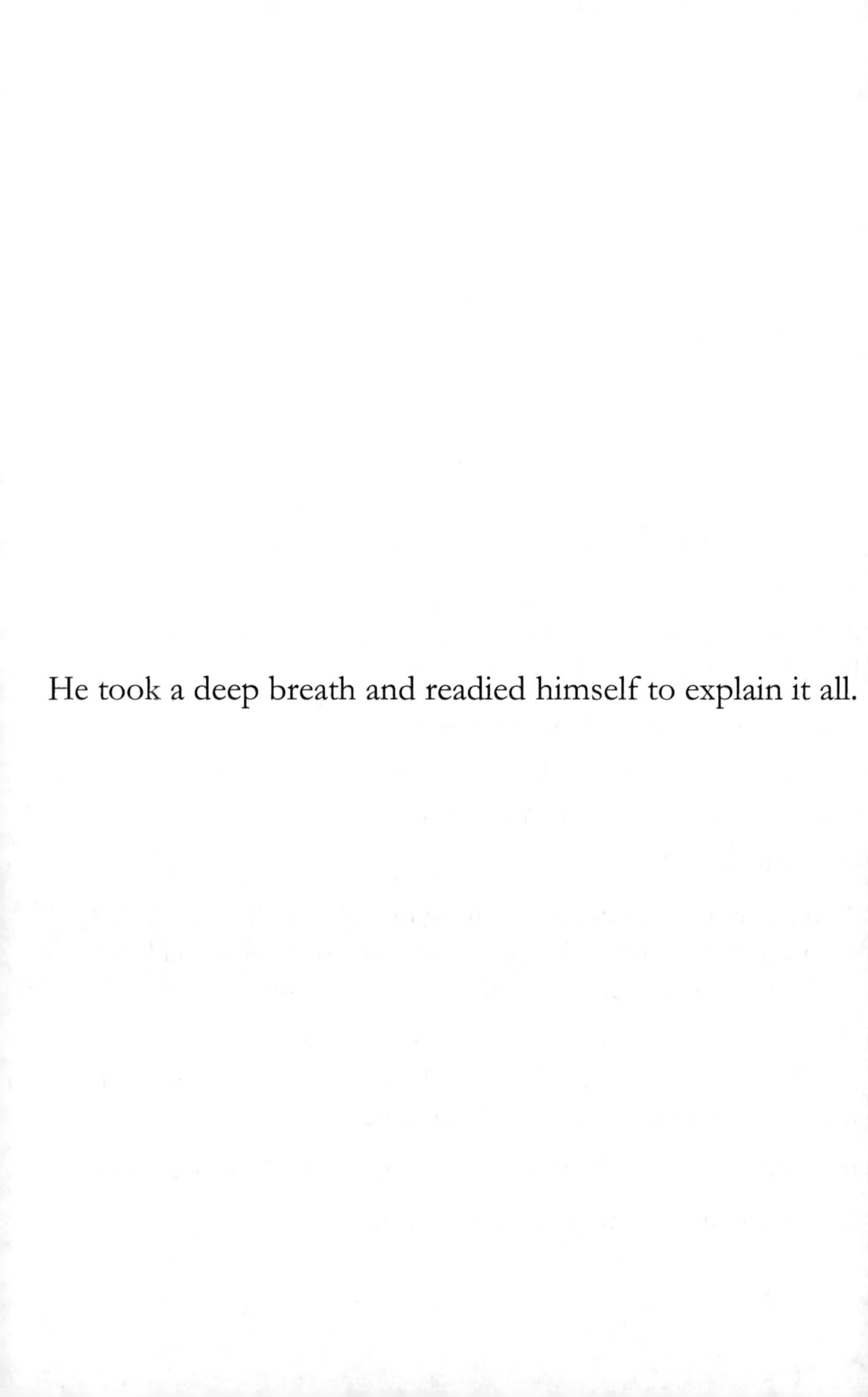

He took a deep breath and readied himself to explain it all.

Taylor was killing her.

It wasn't that she hadn't enjoyed every minute she'd spent with him this evening. She'd not even questioned what his intentions were when he texted, glad for the opportunity to spend the evening with him.

She didn't have a crush on him. That's not what this was about. It had nothing to do with how she thought about his smile when they were apart, how she felt her heart beat a little faster every time she got a text from him, or how she'd been nearly breathless when he'd taken her hand earlier, his eyes meeting hers over the chopsticks.

This wasn't about a crush. He was a friend. And she enjoyed spending time with him, which is why she hadn't wondered what tonight was all about.

Until now.

"Taylor," she said, settling in on his couch, so close to him that their knees touched. "What are you thinking?"

He seemed to be struggling with the best way to tell her what he'd found out.

Oh, no. Was it bad? Had it been another dead end?

Or had it been worse?

How could it be worse?

"Taylor," she said again.

And this prompted him into finally speaking.

"Did you ever have one of those prayer guide apps?" he asked. "You know, one of the ones that would tell you about unreached people groups?"

She had. Her parents had made praying for a different people group every night part of their routine.

What did this have to do with anything?

"I did," she said. "I have one on my phone even now."

Taylor nodded. "Okay, then you know that there are lots of people groups in Asia in particular. In southeast Asia, in central Asia, in south Asia… in east Asia. China alone has billions of people, but the great majority of them are Han. Does any of this make sense?"

Not really, but she nodded anyway.

Why was he talking about all of this?

"Okay," she said, eager for him to get to his point.

"The great majority of the people in China are ethnically Han," he said. "But there are pockets of ethnic minority groups. And to your average American, the differences between them are indistinguishable. As are, unfortunately, the differences between ethnic differences in whole nations. Which is why you've likely spent a good portion of your life being called Japanese, Korean, Indonesian… the list goes on and on."

She nodded because it was true. He really had no idea.

"But when I saw you," he said, "I knew you were Chinese. Because I know what it is to be Chinese. But when you said you were from Shanghai, I was confused because you're clearly not Han. Or any of the other major groups."

Clearly?

"Like I said," Taylor continued on, "I know because I've lived there most of my life. And before then, I was here in the middle of a Chinese community, all of them from those major people groups. And you're not like them, Jade."

How was she not like them? And why did any of this matter?

"I'll have to take your word on it," Jade said, able to count on one hand the Asian people she'd known in her lifetime.

"You don't have to take my word on it," he said. "You can take the word of Laura Hemsworth, the woman who has your records."

What?

"You found my records?" she asked, her voice trembling. "Wait… so my Shanghai records aren't right?"

This was a lot to take in.

"Maybe I should have started off with that," Taylor said thoughtfully.

"You think?" she asked, unable to keep a laugh from escaping. Her heart was pounding. He'd really found something, he knew something –

"So," he said, smiling now, "it all makes good sense, why the way that you looked…" He swallowed now. "Well, it's at least part of the reason why I had to take a moment when we first met."

What had been the other part of that reason? She found herself wondering it as he watched her.

"I know where you're from," he said. "They didn't have official records, but Laura Hemsworth was there when you came to Shanghai and she notated the details. So I know where you were born, what people group you likely belong to, and it makes perfect sense when I look at you… because you look like them."

None of this made any sense to her.

"What does all of this mean for the search for my birth mother?" she asked. "And why was I adopted from Shanghai if I'm from… where? Where am I from?"

This was the question. This is all that mattered.

"The Sichuan province," he said, beaming. "You're from the Sichuan province. It's actually a very cool place. That's where the pandas are! And it's ironic, because they have the spiciest food in China, and you, judging by all the gagging you did earlier, just can't handle it."

She stared at him blankly for a moment, taking it in.

He must have seen it in her eyes, that ethnic classifications and cultural information really wasn't paramount here. No, she needed to know about her birth story, about what had happened –

"Laura confirmed it," he said, "that you're from Chengdu. It's a big city, so it's not the best news for our purposes because there were likely many, many babies born there around the same time you were, making it more difficult to find your birth mother. But the fact that you're not Han… well, that narrows the search down a bit."

"Okay," she said slowly, trying to comprehend this. Chengdu. She knew she'd never be able to find that on a map, that she had no idea where it even was.

Chengdu. She'd been born in Chengdu.

"House of Hope sent a nanny to come and get you there in Chengdu, and once you got to Shanghai, they did all of your paperwork as though you'd been born there, as if you were Han just like everyone else. It's why your parents thought you were Shanghainese all this time. I'm not sure why House of Hope didn't correct them or why your parents didn't ever question it since you don't look traditionally Chinese –"

"They're Americans," Jade said softly. "They were counting themselves as quite worldly when they were able to affirmatively call me Chinese and not Filipino or Cambodian…"

Her parents. God bless them. They'd had no idea what they were doing, who it was they were getting all those years ago.

Taylor smiled at this. "I can see that. And good on them, for knowing what they did, at least. That they were meant to adopt you, to bring you to the States, and to help you with medical care. Your cerebral palsy saved you in a way, because it was the very reason that House of Hope came and got you. Otherwise, if you'd been healthy, you would have stayed in Chengdu and probably never been adopted."

What a thought.

She could barely wrap her mind around that.

But there were still questions.

"Jade," Taylor said, sensing this somehow. "What are you thinking?

He wasn't sure what was going through her mind. It was a lot to take in, all that he'd shared already, but he could see her struggling with something beyond all of the facts and the information he'd relayed.

Sure enough, she raised her eyes to his, even more vulnerability there in her gaze.

"What was the story?" she asked him softly.

"Story?" he asked. "What do you mean?"

"My history didn't start at House of Hope," she said. "Did Laura tell you what happened in… Chengdu?"

He'd known this was coming.

And this was the hard part. He would do his best to make it easier.

"You were from Chengdu," he said carefully. "At a state-run orphanage, where you would have lived out the rest of your childhood, bed bound likely."

That was a heartbreaking thought.

"But that's not what happened," Taylor continued, his voice intentionally brighter now. "Even though you were part of an ethnic minority group and the government would have frowned on it, you had the great fortune of being left at an orphanage with some very caring workers who didn't fear the government like most. They got in touch with the home in Shanghai and made arrangements." He took a breath, shaking his head. "It's like the midwives in Egypt, the ones who protected those baby boys from

Pharaoh. That's what those workers did when they contacted House of Hope and made arrangements for you. You were actually better off than most of the others, because of your cerebral palsy. Without it… House of Hope wouldn't have taken you. So your cerebral palsy saved you in a way."

Wild. Cerebral palsy, something to be thankful for…

But that couldn't be what Jade was thinking.

"But before then, Taylor," she said softly. "I know that I was at House of Hope. And I know now how I got there, thanks to those workers in Chengdu."

She was silent for a long moment.

"But how did I end up at that orphanage?"

Oh, God, help me. Give me the words.

Taylor found himself praying it, praying that God would answer him for Jade's benefit.

"Laura said that when they got the call at House of Hope, the workers at Chengdu told them that you…"

He stopped himself, swallowing, realizing as he said each word that he wasn't speaking about just another child, just one of the statistics. He was speaking about Jade, about those first months of her life.

He took her hands in his, choosing these words carefully.

"You were left on the doorstep," he said. "Wrapped in a blanket. No note. Nothing. They estimated that you were two months old but couldn't be certain, of course. And it took them…"

He just had to say it.

"It took them a while to find you," he said. "It was a Chinese holiday. So they had limited staff. And you were left on a back doorstep, so…"

Jade blinked at this, her eyes full of tears.

God, help me…

"But they found you," he said. "They found you, and they cleaned you up and got you fed. And right from the beginning, they were able to make some good guesses about your cerebral palsy."

Jade took a steadying breath, then nodded for him to continue.

"You were… you weren't able to move like most of the other babies," he said. "And they said that your condition might not have been obvious when you were a newborn. Or that you weren't born in a traditional hospital. That it was possible you were born in a home, that your birth mother had likely assumed you were fine… until you got a little older, which is when she saw that you weren't like other babies."

He could see the conclusions Jade was drawing in her mind, and he could do nothing to stop them.

Because they were likely the right conclusions.

"She left me, then?" she asked softly. "I mean, I've always assumed so, but hearing it like this… she left me because I wasn't like other babies?"

There were tears in her eyes, and Taylor watched, heartbroken himself, as one made its way down her cheek.

"I can understand it, given that she was expecting a whole, perfect child," she said, wiping at it with the back of her hand. "And I wasn't what she wanted."

"Hey," he said, scooting closer to her now as she began to cry in earnest, squeezing her hands. "Maybe it had nothing to do with being wanted. Maybe your birth mother did what she could and made a hard decision to do what was best for you, putting you in a place where the right people could come in and do more for you than she could."

"Maybe," Jade managed, sniffling, her tears still coming.

He'd known this would be hard. Oh, but he wanted to take the pain away from her. He had the thought even as he let go of her hands and pulled her into his arms, gently and naturally. He could feel her begin to cry harder now.

He held her for a long while, not saying anything, just letting her cry as he smoothed out her hair with his hand, rubbing her back comfortingly.

And in time, her sobs ceased and her breathing evened out. Yet Taylor kept his arms around her, still holding her close.

And he said something, something he knew with absolute certainty.

"God never took His eyes off of you," he whispered. "Not for one moment, Jade."

He could say it with confidence. The words of grace came back to him, and though he struggled to believe them for his own life, he knew with certainty that they were true for Jade's. Weren't God's fingerprints all over her story?

"I mean, look at what happened," he said as he held her close, whispering the words over her. "Mark and Molly were praying for you even then, without knowing anything about you, asking God to make them parents. And He did, putting you with them, and that opened the door for all of your surgeries, for your therapy, for your medication… and beyond that, it opened the door for you to be exactly where you are right now."

With me.

That felt right, too.

"In a place where I came to know Christ," Jade said.

Yes, this was more important than her being with him. But still…

"Exactly," he said. "Maybe the things that happened weren't because you were unwanted. But all that has happened since has gone on like it has because you were wanted. By your parents. By God Himself. He made something beautiful out of a very broken situation, and He used your parents in it all."

Something beautiful.

"You're wanted, Jade," he murmured again, thinking about how wonderful and valuable she was. To God, to her parents… to him.

And Jade was quiet for so long that Taylor wondered if she'd heard him.

But then she answered him, the word resonating against his chest and in his heart.

“Amen.”

They had a plan, and in a week's time, they were working at it in earnest, putting together information inquiries side by side in the language lab.

"I've been researching it," Jade had told him just a day after he'd told her about Chengdu. "About others like me, people who want to find their birth parents in China. Did you know that there are websites, whole online communities where there are posting boards where birth parents and children alike can search for one another?"

The news about Chengdu had been a blow to her because she'd finally had it confirmed that she'd been left and abandoned, all likely because of her medical condition. Not that she'd ever doubted the reality of any of this before, but hearing it confirmed had been painful.

Taylor had made it better, though. With his words, with his compassion, with the way he'd held her as she'd cried. And with the way he'd told her that he'd be with her for the next step.

Actually finding her mother.

Taylor had nodded when she'd brought it all up the next day, after they'd sat together in church again, after he'd had lunch with her family and they'd told them what they'd found, and after the two of them had gone back to campus together to get ready for another week of classes. "I stumbled across a few of those very same websites back before we knew we were going to be looking beyond Shanghai," Taylor said. "And I've already been thinking about how to best word yours, what we need to say to get the information to the right person."

He'd already been thinking about it. Of course, he had. Because he'd made all of this his priority as well. If she hadn't believed his investment in this before he told her about Chengdu, there was no doubt in her mind afterwards, not after he'd been so understanding and so gentle.

He was in this with her.

"Here," he said in the language lab, talking quietly over the constant hum of computers as he passed her a notepad with a few of the most important points written out.

Her estimated birthdate. A concise description of her cerebral palsy. A few words about Chengdu, the name of the state-run orphanage where she'd been left. And Taylor's best conclusion about her people group.

"Yes," she said to it all. "I feel like I've double and triple checked this already in all the time you and I have been going over it this week. Maybe even more than that."

"We want to get it exactly right," Taylor agreed. "And here's the Chinese translation."

And there it was, in Taylor's penmanship, all in Chinese characters.

"Wow," she murmured, smiling at it.

"My handwriting is awful, I know," he said.

She widened her eyes, staring at him. "I'm not even sure how I would know," she said. "I'm more impressed that you can do this.

And I wouldn't know the first thing about getting that into a digital format."

She wouldn't have had a clue on her own. How many times had Taylor been just who she needed in this whole process? How many more times would he be the only one who could help her out when it came to finding her birth mother?

She wasn't sure, but even as they sat together and Taylor navigated to the first website where they could post this information, she thanked God for him all over again.

She looked at Taylor, ready to tell him for perhaps the hundredth time how much she appreciated him, only to find that he was watching her as well. That look in his eyes, the way it made her feel, the way she felt like all the world could fall away because she was sitting here with him –

"Taylor?"

That voice broke the gazes that they'd kept on one another. That voice, coming from one of the students who was in the language lab, a student who Jade had seen more than once here, who was always not so subtly flirting with Taylor, trying to get his attention.

She had it now as Taylor got up to help her with her French program. But Taylor was different as he helped her. Subdued. Emotionless. Almost mechanical, even as this girl continued to do her best to get his attention, to cajole him into flirting back with her.

Come to think of it, Jade had seen this kind of thing before. She'd seen it in the music building with other girls, when Taylor found her after her wind ensemble, when he was in between classes. The smiles and the attention he had for her was never a part of his interaction with other girls. And when she'd mused over this, her mind had always gone back to Mindy Crenshaw, to the way he'd looked at her, to what she'd said…

The love you and leave you kind.

She was still thinking on it when Taylor dropped back into the seat next to her, giving her a smile as he did so.

That. That smile. Why was he like this with her but no one else? And why was he so distant and closed off to so many women?

"You ready?" he asked, prompting Jade to look at the website, the message board, where he was getting ready to copy and paste her inquiry.

This was a big deal. A huge deal. A step that would lead to finding her birth mother, hopefully.

But Jade was caught up thinking about Taylor.

"She likes you," she said.

Taylor looked confused for a moment, glancing back to the message board then to Jade.

"What?" he asked.

"Her," Jade said, nodding at the girl, her voice lowered. "She flirts with you every time I'm here. Does she even go to class, or does she spend all of her time here?"

She hoped that didn't sound rude. But honestly…

"Oh," Taylor said. And there it was again. That blankness in his expression.

"Do you not like girls?" she asked.

Only after the words were out of her mouth did she want to pull them back.

What a question.

Taylor looked back at her with surprise in his eyes.

She was about to apologize, but he beat her to it.

"Yes, I do like girls," he said. "But…"

"You don't date?" she asked, figuring if she was asking rude questions already, she should keep on going. And honestly, she was curious. Not for personal reasons. No, she'd wondered about it on Taylor's behalf, about whether or not she was monopolizing his time like this, always with him the way she was, pretty sure there wasn't a girlfriend in the picture but wanting to make absolutely sure.

Not for personal reasons, of course. No, it wasn't –

She sighed. Okay. So it was personal.

She looked at him as he seemed to struggle for the right words.

"It's a long story," he said, still poised to post her information.

Maybe she should focus on what was her business. This search for her birth mother, not getting all into Taylor's personal life.

But they were friends. Good friends and…

He posted her inquiry to the website and sat back, releasing a sigh.

She should have felt euphoric at this. Excited to get this process started. There should have been a burst of anticipation, a moment of her heart warming at all that was up ahead.

But all of her attention was on Taylor.

He took a breath then looked at her.

"Do you have some time tonight to talk?" he said very softly.

She nodded, sensing that he was going to tell her something important, something that he hadn't told anyone before.

"Of course," she said.

And when he told her he'd meet her at her dorm later, she felt that anticipation that had been missing earlier.

She still felt that anticipation later on that evening as she and Taylor walked across the empty campus.

He'd come by earlier, seemingly at a loss for where to begin, so she'd suggested that they take a walk. Though he'd expressed some concern over her walking so much, she'd waved away his words, telling him that it was good for her and that she'd be fine as long as they took it at her pace.

And they had. The slow pace and the fresh air seemed to help Taylor to find the right words.

"You asked about the girl in the language lab," he said. "And about whether or not I date."

"I shouldn't have asked such personal questions," she said. "You don't have to tell me anything."

"How could it be too personal when I know so much about you?" he asked.

What was good for the gander was good for the goose, yes, but it didn't seem right in this case.

But Taylor glanced over at her, his expression vulnerable.

"You don't have to tell me the details, Taylor," she said softly.

She didn't need to know them. She knew him now, knew what God was doing in his heart and what He'd done in his life.

That was enough.

"I want to tell you, though," he said just as softly. "I want you to know everything about me, Jade."

Wow. Jade had hardly been able to grasp the significance of that before he started telling her his story.

"I made some big mistakes my first year back in the States," he said softly, looking out over campus as they walked. "I came here thinking that I was going to do big things for God. And then, it was hard, I was lonely, and it was…" He took a breath. "It was foreign."

"This town?" she asked, imagining that it had to have been.

"Everything," he sighed. "This place, this culture, college life, being away from home, from my church…"

Jade hadn't had that experience. Maybe her parents were clingier than some, though they'd done a great job of doing their best to let her go. Jade had never appreciated their clinginess, their nearness before.

But hearing Taylor talk about his own sense of loss in being alone had her reconsidering it.

"Fitting in here, especially in the music department, meant embracing the culture, to a certain extent," he said.

She knew this. She'd watched Olivia steadily grow more and more enmeshed into the culture of the music majors, forming friendships and relationships that were natural and easy because of all the connections they shared. It wasn't just a social thing, either. There were professional connections to be had in mingling with the older students, with the graduate level musicians. Networking, not unlike Jade found herself doing in the chemistry department with the pre-pharmacy crowd.

But it was different with the musicians. It was like its own culture over there.

"It wasn't a big deal at first," he said. "Going to parties, hanging out with everyone else. I could still be a light for Christ. I should have been a light for Christ. But that — being like that — set me apart, made it even harder to fit in. And after a while…"

It was too much.

"You wanted to fit in," she said. "And who you were changed."

"Who I was must not have been grounded in Christ," he said, shrugging. "Because I fell so quickly."

Jade wasn't sure about that, wasn't sure what words she could use to counter what he believed, what he thought about his lack of faith then and now —

"I was with quite a few girls," he said very plainly. "I was living like the rest of the world and feeling very little conviction for doing so. And as it turns out, when I was living like the world, I wasn't even a nice guy under the worldliness. I used and dismissed girls without a second thought. That's who I was without Christ. Who I really am."

His expression was hard as he said it, and the words took Jade's breath away. Not for what he'd done but for the truth of what he'd just said.

That's who I was without Christ. Who I really am.

The love you and leave you kind.

"Is that why Mindy Crenshaw hates you?" she asked, unable to keep from asking the question.

"Mindy Crenshaw among others," he said with a sigh. "And it only got worse when I finally came to my senses and cut myself off completely from the whole mess. I stopped going to the parties, stopped hanging out with everyone outside of class, and disappeared off the radar for a while."

"Because you were convicted?"

"Yes," he said. "That's part of it. And I started wondering if I was making the right choice for the future. With music, with education…"

Interesting.

"Are the two connected?" she asked. "Do you think maybe you feel unsettled about the future and your career because it's somehow tied to your experiences that first year?"

She could tell that he'd considered it but not lingered on the idea.

"Maybe," he said softly.

More than maybe. If he'd stayed true to Christ, if he'd walked in godliness while jumping into those classes and into that career path, he'd likely feel very different about the future.

And what was more, Christ could redeem it all for him. He'd walked away, but had he really allowed himself to rest in the grace that was his?

Oh, Taylor…

"You think less of me," he said very simply. "And I understand that."

"I don't think less of you," she said, shaking her head. "I think more of you, that you walked away from the way you'd been living, even though it came at a cost to you."

He nodded, his shoulders slumped forward.

"Hey," she said, reaching out and putting her hand to his arm. "Taylor, look at me."

He raised his eyes to hers, and she could see the remorse there.

So much remorse, so much guilt, so much that he was still carrying even all this time later.

"You've put it all into the hands of Jesus," she said. "Don't grab it back from Him. Leave it with Him. He can handle it."

"I know He can," Taylor said. "But you don't understand the kind of guy I was —"

"Jesus was there, He knows," Jade said. "And it doesn't change anything."

Oh, that he might understand.

"You don't have to be who you were," she said. "You aren't who you were. And you don't have to be tied to that past forever. There is no condemnation for those who are in Christ." She smiled. "No more for you, Taylor Robinson. Rejoice in that and move past it all."

And even as she said goodbye to him later that night, she prayed that he would.

The more sites they posted to, the more information they got back.

He and Jade spent hours together looking over it all, perusing all the tips they got from people in Chengdu, dismissing the outright junk mail, and struggling to read the tearful letters from Chinese mothers looking for their birth children.

None of the dates matched up. None of the medical conditions were Jade's. Oh, but there was still such hope as these women reached out to her.

Jade remained hopeful as well. If there were so many searching out there, perhaps her mother was searching as well. Jade was always optimistic, just as she'd been when she'd told him that he could let go of his past.

He was believing it more and more, especially after his meeting with Mark a few weeks later.

"We want you to go to China with Jade," Mark said as soon as Taylor was sitting in the seat across from the pastor's desk.

This certainly wasn't what Taylor had been expecting when the church secretary had called him earlier and asked him to come by. No, he'd expected this to be a meeting with the children's minister and that it would be about the background check forms he'd had to fill out for one of the children's ministry events he was going to help Jade with at Christmas. He knew searching his records back farther than his return to the US would be difficult since he'd been in China, and he suspected that the children's minister needed better details.

When he'd gotten to the church, though, the secretary had directed him to Mark's office.

And the topic was Jade's trip to China.

Mark and Molly had already started anticipating it, Jade had told him, the money saved and ready for when she found her birth mother. All three of them were going to go and experience China together.

Or not.

"But I… I don't understand," Taylor said, even as his heart gave a hopeful leap at the thought of being with Jade during this next step of her journey, of seeing home through her eyes, and getting to experience this huge moment of her life beside her.

He shouldn't want these moments with her. He should want more for Jade than a guy like him…

But his heart certainly couldn't be convinced. It hadn't been convinced during all these months of knowing her.

He shook his head, focusing on what was most important now. Jade. Going to China. Going to China with… him?

"Why do you want me to go to China with her?" he asked Mark. "Wouldn't it be better if she went with you and Molly?"

Mark took a deep breath. "We would have thought so," he said. "And we did, years ago when we adopted Jade. We always planned on taking her back when she was a young adult. A cultural trip, letting her see the sights, experience it all, and just be there where she was born. And we figured that we would be right by her side through all of it." He shrugged. "That said, she met you, and as it turns out, you've changed everything we thought we knew. We didn't even have her birthplace right, come to find out. And we didn't do a great job of helping her grasp the culture either, as I'm sure you've found out. Jade doesn't eat Chinese food. Did you know that?"

Taylor couldn't keep from smiling at this, remembering the way Jade had giggled and gagged through that meal at his apartment the night that he'd told her about Chengdu.

"We weren't counting on you when this all started," Mark kept on. "When Jade wanted to know about her birth mother. And through it all, through all that she's been learning about her past this year, we've seen her grow a lot, and we know that a great part of that has been because of you."

This was too kind of him. There was so much he didn't know about Taylor…

"And then there are the practical aspects," he said. "You know the country. You know the areas she'll be traveling to. You know the language. Clearly you're better equipped to help her to get where she's going. And once she's there…" Mark shook his head.

"Yes, sir?" Taylor asked.

"Well," he said, choosing his words carefully, "I think there's a joy that you bring to her. A joy that she might need as she asks herself some hard questions in all of this. It's not an easy thing, the questions Jade has about the past. And I think that having you there when she gets all of her answers… well, I think that you're going to help her."

He would do his best. He would do everything in his power to help Jade, to take care of her, to bring her joy.

But could he do this? He wasn't who she needed, no matter what he wanted.

"And I think," Mark said, studying him, "that she's going to help you, Taylor."

Taylor could feel his pulse pick up as the other man watched him knowingly.

"What do you mean, sir?"

"I know this will be your first trip back," he said. "That you've been away from home for three years now. That's a long time to go, to be apart from your family. And I'm guessing that there are reasons why. And as your pastor…" He shrugged. "Can I call myself your pastor, Taylor?"

Taylor nodded, thankful for these past weeks and all that the Matthews family had become to him. "Yes. Of course."

"Well, as your pastor, I have some guesses as to why that is, that you haven't been back home."

Taylor hoped not. And yet at the same time, he hoped Mark understood some of what he was going through. It would be a comfort for someone to understand, to have someone walk through this with him, someone to counsel him.

Someone other than Jade, who believed in him too much, who had made it sound so easy when she'd told him to leave his past in the hands of Jesus.

Mark would tell it to him straight, tell him that it wasn't enough to be repentant and sorry for his sin.

Maybe it was okay to be transparent, to be honest with him.

"My parents are missionaries," he said very simply. "I mean, not officially. They can't officially be missionaries in China, but…"

He trailed off.

Mark smiled. "I gathered as much."

"Right," Taylor said. "And so I know all about Jesus, all about what He did. I made a decision to follow Him when I was really young, and my parents did the work of discipling me as I grew up. My pastor in China did as well, as I got ready to leave home and come to the US for school."

That had been the turning point.

"I made a lot of mistakes when I first came to the US," Taylor said softly. "And it's probably not that different than most students who go away to college, who experience some freedom in that first year away from home. Parties with alcohol, some drugs… lots of girls…"

It was hard, saying these things. He'd lived it all out loud, pretending even then that it didn't prick his conscience, but saying it here with this pastor had him feeling even more repentant than he had in these last difficult years when he'd known that he couldn't atone for his sins.

"Most people wouldn't feel so much guilt," Taylor said. "But I wasn't like most kids when I started college. I came to the US thinking that I was going to be a missionary here, that God was going to use me to change the world. And I really believed it. Really prayed toward that end, before I even left China. And then I got here and…"

It was hard. It was lonely. It was a real struggle, finding myself at that age, in my new context, in a completely different culture…

"I felt lost," he said softly. "And there was a season in time when all the words that Christ said somehow weren't as comforting. They couldn't fill the lonely hours. Maybe that was a lack of faith on my part. Or maybe it just showed how shallow my walk was. I don't know. But when it came to a choice to follow Christ and hold steadfastly to Him or to have friends around me, even if having those friendships meant compromising my standards, I didn't hesitate long in making that choice."

Mark nodded. "Your story isn't so unusual, Taylor," he said softly. "You know that, right? That this happens. That we all stumble, we all fall."

Not as spectacularly. And not with as little remorse as Taylor had.

"I was glad about it all," Taylor said. "At the time, I mean. It wasn't like I was unwillingly doing all that I did. I enjoyed myself. I partied hard, really embraced the kind of lifestyle that I knew was wrong. And I turned my back on God, knowing exactly what I was doing."

Mark continued to listen.

"I was a bad guy," Taylor said softly. "A really bad guy. Not the kind of guy you'd want your daughter with, sir."

There. That was the truth.

"You were a bad guy," Mark repeated. "Taylor, you *are* a bad guy. So am I. There are none who are righteous. Not one."

"I know that," Taylor said, remembering it vaguely from scripture, from the lessons his parents had taught him over the years. "But there's a difference between being a good guy and sinning now and then and being a horrible guy who sins without any kind of guilt or repentance either one."

"I think you're the guiltiest man I've ever met," Mark said very succinctly. "I see you squirm when I preach. Squirm and still listen like the very words I'm saying are life."

Taylor did this. He knew he did.

"That's indicative of repentance on its own," Mark said. "And couple that with the way that you no longer live like you did."

"How do you know that?" Taylor asked.

"Because you spend all of your free time with Jade," Mark said.

That was the truth. And before then, Taylor had walked away from his partying lifestyle. It made him a lonely man in the music department, but he preferred that to what he'd had before.

"And I know it because I see it, in the way you've treated Jade, the way you've been so kind and good to her, the way she says you show such strength of character every time you come up against a roadblock in helping her… well, it's all fruit of a repentant heart."

Could it be?

"You're forgiven, Taylor," Mark said. "God forgave you the moment you acknowledged that He alone could do it and that you were in sore need of it."

"But I don't deserve forgiveness," Taylor said. "Because I knew better when I went out and did all that I did."

That was the heart of the problem. He didn't deserve forgiveness because he'd sinned willingly. It was one thing to live like the devil when you didn't know any different, but to do so when you knew right from wrong…

He didn't deserve forgiveness. He'd never be able to earn it.

"And so the righteousness of Christ is no longer imputed to you because you haven't earned it?" Mark asked. "Is that what you're saying?"

Taylor hesitated. Yes, that's what he was saying. That's what he believed, honestly.

But the words Mark used. The words he'd taught.

Taylor had a realization. Finally.

"That's not biblical," he said.

And like that, something clicked.

Mark smiled. "You're right," he said. "It's not biblical. So why are you believing it?"

"I'm not," Taylor said, uncomfortable at this realization, at the truth that he had been believing it this whole time, holding the grace of Christ at arm's length because he hadn't earned it.

As if he could ever earn it.

He still believed it in a conflicted part of his heart, even as he denied it.

"I think you do, though," Mark said thoughtfully. "But here's the truth, Taylor. A truth I think you've known in your head for the great majority of your life. A truth that maybe now, you're ready to know in your heart."

Taylor readied himself for it.

"We don't earn the grace of God, the righteousness of Christ," Mark said. "That's given to us freely, no matter what we've done."

"But it matters what we do," Taylor said.

"What we do isn't what saves us," Mark corrected him. "Because there's no way you could do enough good to cover over all the bad you've done. You're looking at this from our perspective where good can outweigh bad. But any bad in God's sight is past redemption. We can't do anything to save ourselves, to redeem the wrongs we've done. That's why we need Christ. That's why God had to do the redeeming Himself. Because we're helpless. You're helpless, Taylor. You can't redeem any of the mistakes you've made. You can't earn that forgiveness. Only God can earn it for you. Only your debtor can pay your debts."

Taylor got that, was beginning to understand it in a new way.

But the way he lived from here on out – it mattered. How could he reconcile this – the need to live a godly life and do the right things – against the truth of grace, which required nothing but faith and that itself was given by God and not of his own doing?

Mark seemed to understand right where he was.

"It's all grace," he said softly. "And once we're there, once Christ has redeemed us and bought us and is transforming us each and every day, we can see things rightly. Our good works don't save us, Taylor. But because we're saved, we'll do good works."

This. This was helpful.

"And by God's grace," Mark kept on, "when we mess up — because we're going to mess up — we'll be forgiven again. Again and again, as you're being sanctified to be more like Christ, as you stumble and fall, even knowing better, you'll be forgiven again. Not by your works but by grace. Grace that will lead you to strive for more, to be more like Jesus and less like you."

"I should already know all of this," he said.

And Mark smiled. "I think you know it with both your mind and your heart now," he said. "And that's going to make all the difference."

Maybe it would.

~Jade~

"Give me another one."

Jade shook her head with a smile, looking up from the laptop before her and the textbooks laid out beside her on Taylor's sofa, only to find him staring at her and smiling back as he continued to strum his guitar.

He'd changed. God had been doing something big in his heart over the last few weeks. He'd joined her church, and the conversations he had with her parents over lunch each week were deeper than they'd been, evidence that he was growing so rapidly, coming back to a faith that had never left, even when he was in the wilderness. She'd seen evidence of it as they'd continued sifting through all of the responses she got to her inquiries, taking her hands in his when the volume of misdirected letters was almost as great as the frustration she felt over wondering if her birth mother would ever find her, his voice soothing yet authoritative as he prayed for her.

And then there were nights like this one, where she came to his apartment to study, away from the loud dorms. He told her that she'd have peace and quiet, that he had to study for his own finals.

Of course, the great majority of his finals were music performance finals.

Yes, he'd changed his major from education to performance.

"It'll only add a year onto my studies," he'd told Jade when he'd looked into it before making the change.

"An extra year," she'd said thoughtfully. "Are you okay with that?"

"Well," he'd shrugged, "it'll mean reapplying for more financial aid and probably working a couple of jobs this summer beyond the language lab so that I can afford another year."

It wouldn't come without cost, making the change. Metaphorically speaking and literally, with two more semesters of tuition to be paid if his financial aid didn't come through.

Taylor had considered this, of course. It was one of his major hesitations.

"But," he'd said, smiling at her, "it means I'll have more time here."

With her.

She knew what he meant without him saying it out loud.

And, oh the change for Taylor now that he'd switched. Gone were the discouraging education classes, and now all he had was his music.

Which was why she couldn't study. He kept interrupting her, taking requests long after she'd stopped offering them without him prompting her to do so, and playing so perfectly, so sweetly, that she found it hard to concentrate at all.

It wasn't just that he kept talking. He'd been an attractive guy before, most definitely… but there was something about him playing music, watching her, that look in his eyes.

Taylor Robinson was hot.

"Come on, Jade," he murmured.

"Itsy Bitsy Spider!" she managed, feeling flushed at the thoughts she was having. "I can't even think of any more songs, Taylor. You've gone and played every last one I could think of while I've been attempting to wrap my mind around organic chemistry, which is –"

"The yueqin," he said, putting his guitar back in its place and reaching for the Chinese instrument, strumming once with his head cocked to the side, one eye squinted, then reaching up to twist the knobs at the top before strumming again.

All by ear. The tuning, the playing, the on the spot composition, just like that.

He was talented. Immensely so. She wasn't sure what kind of work was out there for musicians, but if it was a competitive field, he would surely come out on top.

"And here we go," he murmured, beginning to play… well, the Itsy Bitsy Spider. But he was doing it with great flare, making faces at her as he did so as though he was some hard-core Chinese rock star.

"You're so weird," she managed, laughing despite herself at this silly side of him, something that had been missing until recently.

Maybe this was the real Taylor. She'd liked the hurting, guarded one just fine, honestly.

But this one… she really, really liked him.

"We need to get you a xiao," he said.

"What's a xiao?" she asked, very nearly closing her book now, convinced that she wouldn't get any work done here with him in this mood that he was in.

"It's like a flute," he said. "A Chinese transverse flute. You're better equipped to play it with your years of American flute experience." He stopped strumming for a second. "Though your flute is Japanese made. Did you know that?"

"All I know right now is that I'm going to fail all of my finals if you don't stop talking," she said.

But she couldn't keep from smiling even as she said it. She wouldn't fail them, but teasing him about how much he was talking was just part of this flirty banter that had become the norm in their relationship lately.

Just like the feelings that flooded her as Taylor put the yueqin up and made his way to the couch, sitting down beside her.

"Let me help, then," he said, pulling her laptop closer, waking the screen back up to see what she was focusing on.

"Do you know anything about organic chemistry?" she asked, grimacing when the work came up, taunting her with its difficulty.

"Chemistry," he said. "I took it in high school. I'm guessing that this is far more advanced than what I know."

"Maybe a little," she agreed. "But the basics are probably the same."

"Any notecards or questions I can use to quiz you?" he asked. "Come on, let me help."

She looked at him, no longer annoyed by all the distractions. Not that she'd been all that annoyed to begin with, as she'd loved every second here with him.

He smiled at her. "What?" he asked.

"Tell me what you know about chemistry," she said, preparing herself for the most basic explanations.

There was a smile tugging at the corners of his lips. "Give me a second. It's been a while. And what I know, I know in Mandarin, so…"

"Translate it in your head," she said. "All about chemistry."

And he looked to be doing just that. But then, his gaze shifted just slightly, taking in the entirety of her face, his own expression softening.

Jade felt the flutters in her stomach start up all over again as she noted that he was leaning closer now.

"Chemistry," he said softly. "Maybe it doesn't need a translation."

"Oh?" she asked, hearing the hoarseness in her voice, her nerves and her desires all tangled up as Taylor was close enough that she could feel his breath on her lips.

"Jade," he said, his hand coming up to her face now, tenderly, reverently. "Chemistry… it's just this thing between people."

And she couldn't help but smile at this, at the flippant explanation, at how it had nothing to do with the subject at hand… at the way that she understood what he really meant.

"Yeah?" she asked, willing him to come closer. "Makes sparks fly, huh?"

He was smiling, too.

Did what they have need no words? No defining?

She sure wondered as he gazed at her, no smile now, only sincerity and genuine affection, his eyes on her lips.

"Jade," he murmured again. She closed her eyes, waiting for it, knowing that his lips on hers would be perfection.

And that's when her computer buzzed at her.

And that tone. It was the email Taylor had set up specifically for the inquiries.

Her eyes flew open, only to find that Taylor was still looking at her, his hand still to her cheek.

He swallowed. "Do you want to…?"

Kiss? Yes, please.

But Taylor's eyes had gone to her laptop, his hand dropping slowly from her face.

Ugh.

Oh, well, they could get back to that. They *would* get back to that, she promised herself.

"Go ahead and check it," she said, needing a few seconds to compose herself.

So Taylor did, leaning over and clicking through to the new message, opening it up and murmuring.

"Mandarin."

"Of course," she said, thinking about how much she'd needed him this whole time and how it hadn't changed as messages poured in and he had to translate them all. They were messages that led nowhere, but what a help it had been to have him translate each and every one of them and then to be there to comfort her when it was just another dead end.

He was so good to her. So, so good.

He would be good to her and help her with this newest disappointment, with this message, with another roadblock –

"Jade."

There was something in his voice that gave her pause.

"What?" she said, following his gaze to the message. "What does it say?"

She couldn't read a word. Not a single one. But she felt the hair on the back of her neck stand up.

Taylor took a breath.

"I think we found your mother, Jade."

Christmas had been different.

Most Christmas holidays in the States had found Taylor visiting distant relatives. His mother had three brothers and two sisters, and if his grandparents, Scott and Marie, hadn't fought them all for the right to have Taylor at their home for Christmas, he would have likely spent the holiday going from one house to another, with bustling family celebrations all around him, finding it easy to hide away. As it was, though, he'd had one subdued Christmas after another with his grandparents, who were so godly that he'd had a difficult time feeling like he could breathe around their discernment, knowing that they knew something wasn't right with him. He'd even overheard the two of them praying for him one night during the last Christmas he spent with them, asking God to grab onto him and change everything.

Oh, this Christmas would have been different. If he had spent it at their house, sharing with them what God had done in his heart, how he'd felt the redemptive work of Christ at work in the last few months, it would have been different. Because he was different, was seeing life differently, and was looking towards a future that was going to be more than he'd dreamt it could be.

God was good. So, so good.

His grandparents had gotten that as he'd talked to them, and they'd rejoiced to hear it. And they'd been supportive when he told them why his plans for Christmas were going to be different.

"A girl, huh?" Scott had asked knowingly. "You're blowing us off to spend Christmas with a girl?"

"Not just any girl, Gramps," he'd said, smiling in spite of himself. "This one is… special."

"She sounds like she is," Marie had sighed appreciatively. "We're glad for that, Taylor."

"And we'll be in Houston a couple of weeks before Christmas," he'd added. "Jade will need to go to the Chinese embassy to get her visa processed for our trip."

They'd done that, taking the piles of paperwork required for American citizens, then another handful of documents on top of that, requirements for Chinese born Americans. What a joy it had been to take Jade to the embassy, where she'd cheerfully and tentatively submitted it all. What a joy it had been to go to his grandparents' suburb afterwards, spending a couple of days at their house, letting Jade get to know them while they waited for her visa to be approved. What a joy, watching Jade study the document in her passport, right before she looked up at him with a wide grin.

"This is really going to happen," she'd said as he'd grinned back.

A couple of weeks later as he spent Christmas at the Matthews home, he felt as though he'd never stop grinning. There was the moment that Mark and Molly opened up the gift he'd made them, a framed print of the Shanghai skyline with each of their names printed in Chinese characters.

Mark. Molly. Jade.

Molly didn't know to be unimpressed with his poor penmanship, so overcome by the memories of those fateful days she'd spent in Shanghai that all she'd been able to manage were watery tears and sobs.

Taylor had felt nearly the same as they'd given him his gift. An erhu, one of the Chinese instruments that he'd long wanted to try out. He'd been overcome by their thoughtfulness, their kindness to him, in bringing him into their family and their fellowship.

It had only made him more emotional when Jade had given him her gift – a whole stack of music sheets, blank and empty.

"Maybe the best songs of your life have yet to be written," she'd said, smiling almost shyly at him. Kind of like the smile that she'd given him as he'd passed along the gift he had for her, long after her parents had gone on to sleep and she and Taylor stayed in the living room, with him trying out that erhu.

"Listen to this," he'd said. And with the bow in one hand and the erhu held tenderly in the other, he began to play a happy little tune, upbeat and sweet.

Jade had shifted in her seat, pulling her knees up, wrapping her arms around them and laying her head to the side, watching him as he continued on for several minutes, playing the song he heard in his head, filling the room with his music.

"It's so different from my yueqin," he'd said. "The bow… it involves an entirely new skill set."

"They didn't know the difference," Jade had said softly, smiling at him, at the music he'd made. "My parents, that is. They didn't know the difference between the erhu and the yueqin. They were just excited that they found something Chinese, so you could, to quote my mother, 'play your Chinese country music.'"

"And it was the best gift," he said. "It's not a bad thing that I'm being stretched to pick up new skills." He lowered his voice. "And I feel like I need to do well with this, to impress my pastor."

She smiled even more at this. "I think that ship has already sailed," she said. "I mean, he's sending you to China with me next week."

Next week.

She'd shaken her head at that. "Next week…"

"It's going to be good," he'd reassured her. "And your mother… Xiu. It's going to be good."

Yes, that inquiry had been simple but powerful.

Her name was Xiu. Her child's birthdate was very close to what they'd estimated Jade's was. And her baby girl, too, had been left near the same location in Chengdu.

There had been more from Xiu – regret that she'd left her child, grief over all the time she'd lost, and a plea to hear from her again. Jade and Taylor had sent back messages. Back and forth they'd communicated with Xiu.

And now they were going to meet her.

Taylor had been able to feel the apprehension and anticipation in Jade's heart, so he'd chosen that moment to give her the gift he'd gotten her, hoping that it would reassure her, would communicate to her that he was here for her.

"Merry Christmas," he'd murmured, pulling it from his pocket and holding it out to her.

A ring box. Jade's eyes had widened, and for a moment, Taylor had wondered if he'd made a miscalculation.

Did she think that he was proposing?

He wasn't, but… well, he would, one day.

What a crazy thought. What an amazing thought.

Before he could clarify, Jade had opened the box, and her breath had caught.

"Jade," she'd said softly.

A jade stone in a silver setting. Simple and elegant. Lovely and fitting.

She'd put it on her finger and wiped away tears.

"Praise God for you, Taylor," she'd whispered. "I'm going to be okay no matter what happens in China, because you're going to be with me."

He would have taken the moment to kiss her — finally — but he'd hesitated after that, moved by the emotion, letting the moment be what it was.

Enough. It was enough.

And there were more moments that next week as they went to the airport, ready to begin their great adventure.

The emotion of the trip began early, with tears from Molly and Mark both as they'd dropped the two of them off at departures for their fourteen hour flight to Shanghai. As they stood with their arms around both Taylor and Jade and prayed, Jade crying with them, Taylor had prayed for them, for their hearts in all of this.

"I'll take care of her," Taylor had reassured Mark in a hushed tone as Molly and Jade had embraced one more time, crying freely with one another.

"I know you will," Mark had said, patting him on the back. "And she'll take care of you."

What a gift Jade had given to him when she'd invited him into her family the way that she had.

Miles and miles and an ocean later, Taylor was able to do the same as they arrived in Shanghai, took a train out to his parents' side of town, and saw the two of them standing in the station waiting for them.

"Jade," he'd said to her, her hand in his, her eyes wide as she took in the crowds and the rush of China's busiest city, "these are my parents, Owen and Hannah."

"Jade," Hannah had said, embracing the younger woman immediately. "Oh, it's so good to meet you." Her eyes had moved to Taylor. "And you," she'd said, her voice breaking. "Taylor, you've grown into a man since I last saw you."

A man he wasn't ashamed for his parents to know, he'd told himself, thankful for what God had done in his life, as he hugged both of his parents.

Then, it was a whirlwind of an introduction to Shanghai, with Jade unable to manage much besides an occasional "wow" and "unbelievable" as they rushed back through the city, his mother pointing out everything as they made their way back to the Robinson home.

"It's big, I know," Hannah had said reassuringly. "There's so much to take in."

"And we can take our time doing so because we've got a few days here before we head to Chengdu," Taylor had said to Jade. "I've got so many places I want to show you –"

"Actually," Owen had said, "you're traveling again tomorrow."

Taylor had frowned, looking between his two parents, watching how they grinned knowingly.

"Jade has to see the sights, Taylor," Hannah had said. "You'll be back here after Chengdu, before you head back to the States. So here at the beginning of the trip, we thought you might like to go somewhere else."

Taylor had tilted his head at this, wondering what they'd done.

"We booked a trip to Beijing," Hannah said, grinning. "We thought you'd like to take Jade to the Forbidden City, the Temple of Heaven, the Great Wall –"

"Oh," Jade had breathed, her hand to her heart. "Oh…"

"Merry Christmas," Hannah had said, squeezing her knee.

"I thought you said your parents weren't very original," Jade had said to Taylor.

And that was the perfect ice breaker, making for an evening full of conversations, stories, and prayers, as Hannah prayed over Jade, prayed for Xiu, and thanked God for what He was going to do.

Taylor had watched Jade leave to go to bed that evening, feeling as content as he ever had.

So, so content.

"You love that girl," Owen had said, studying him. "And I think she loves you, too."

"It's too soon for all of that," Taylor said, brushing this off even as he longed for it to be true. Not that he didn't love her – because he was certain that he did. But surely it was impossible that she could have begun to love him, despite him, in this short time.

"Is it?" Owen asked.

And Taylor, just as he was about to deny it again, thinking about Jade and all the happiness she'd brought to his life, found that he couldn't do anything but smile.

~Jade~

Jade felt like she could hardly catch her breath.

China had been a whirlwind so far. From the moment their plane had touched down in Shanghai, Jade had been dumbfounded by the rush of life around them. In immigration, going through packed lines full of people all chatting in a language that was still unfamiliar to her, with Taylor holding her hand and speaking easily for her in his soothing, comforting Mandarin. Waiting for the train to whisk them from the airport to his parents' neighborhood, squished in with others, holding onto a support pole as she stared at the skyscrapers and the distinctive skyline, Taylor's arm around her protectively as he pointed each one out by name. Then with his parents, as they'd brought her into their home, all of them chatting over one another and filling up the absence left by the three years that Taylor had been away, as she sat on the couch with Ling, Taylor's brother's giant dog, staring at her plaintively, his massive head in her lap as she could still hear the bustle of traffic outside, motorbikes and taxis, buses and trucks, honking and bleating into the Shanghai night.

It was overwhelming. China was overwhelming. All that she felt here in this place was overwhelming.

"I'm here," she'd told her parents on the phone that night, hardly able to catch her breath. "We made it."

"Has Shanghai changed much since we were last there?" Molly asked eagerly, excitement in her voice. Then, with a laugh, "Listen to me. How would you even remember, right?"

Jade had smiled and shaken her head. "I don't remember, but it's a safe bet that Shanghai has changed a lot, I'm sure. And tomorrow, I'm taking a train to Beijing with Taylor and his parents."

Yes, Hannah – who was a travel agent by trade – had shared with them all of the details, and Jade had found herself unable to catch her breath yet again when she'd heard that they were going to see each and every spot she thought they wouldn't get to.

"Not this trip, at least," Taylor had told her weeks ago back in the US when they'd planned it all. "We'll be in Shanghai and Chengdu for the entirety of this trip. But next time, I'll take you to Beijing. Maybe Guilin. Or Xi'an." He'd smiled. "We're going to have to make lots of trips actually. China is huge."

We. Jade hadn't missed the unspoken implication. It had left her breathless, knowing that Taylor was placing himself in her future, that he was planning on being with her for much longer than just this trip, than just this season.

This season, which began early the next morning on a high-speed train from Shanghai to Beijing, side by side with Taylor, his parents sitting across the aisle. From there, Hannah was in tour guide mode, taking them from one stop to the next, filling Jade in on the history of each place as she did so. They started the day at Tiananmen Square, where they didn't speak of what had happened in that significant place, but Jade had seen it in her mind as Taylor had squeezed her hand in his. Then, they went into the Forbidden City, with Hannah telling her about the history, about the emperors and the dynasties of the Chinese people, with Jade blinking back tears at the realization that this was her history, too. She'd smiled in spite of herself as Chinese tourists had wanted to pose for pictures with Taylor, the foreigner, never guessing that Jade was the foreign one here, even though she looked like one of them.

One of them. For the first time in her life, Jade was like everyone around her. Except not, because she was breathless at it all, as they took a taxi over to the Lama Temple, with incense burning around them, with people offering up prayers to a god that didn't hear them.

She was different. If life hadn't gone the way it had, if she hadn't been unwanted, would she have ever heard the gospel? Would God have found her and sought her and bought her despite it all?

What a thought.

On their second day in Beijing, Jade kept all of these thoughts close to her heart as they walked the streets of the hutongs, trying out food again and again with Taylor failing to bite back one grin after another as Jade braved every crazy, exotic bite. She was starting to feel the effects of jet lag and napped on Taylor's shoulder on the drive up to the Mutianyu section of the Great Wall, wide awake once they got there, once they headed up on what looked to be a ski lift, and when she finally saw the wall.

They spent the afternoon walking and exploring, gazing down at the countryside and posing for pictures, and by the time the sun began to set, Jade was feeling all the physical exertion that she'd spent over the last two days.

She was breathless. And dragging her leg more than she wanted to admit or wanted anyone to notice. She was thankful when Hannah and Owen split away from them, going to get some pictures at one of the lower sections of the wall, leaving her alone with Taylor.

"I think I'm done," she told him as he continued to climb, her hand in his.

He stopped and turned to her, concern in his eyes. Then, realization. "Oh, Jade, I didn't even think about —"

"I'm glad you didn't," she said, meaning this entirely. "You've gotten so good at taking things at my pace that I think you forget that you're compensating for me."

And that I can't do as much as you can.

"I was just having a good time with you," he said apologetically, holding her hands in his now as he faced her, smiling.

"Me, too, Taylor," she said.

"And there was a spot I wanted to show you," he said, glancing up to where he'd been heading all along.

"I don't think I can make it up there," she said. "Not if you want me to make it back down to the van. And even that… I'm struggling."

"Here, then," he said, reaching out and picking her up, holding her in his arms, even as she gasped at the surprise of him doing so. "I'll carry you."

It was romantic and chivalrous. And impossible, she noted, when Taylor stopped after a hundred yards or so of carrying her in his arms, breathless himself.

"I'm too heavy," she said, unable to keep from laughing. "I blame all that weird food you had me eating earlier."

"It's not that you're heavy, because you're not," he said, putting her down. "It's that carrying you like that has me off center or something." He thought for a moment then turned around, squatting down. "Hop on my back."

"You're going to give me a piggyback ride up the Great Wall?" she asked, amused at the mental image.

"Is there any other way to be escorted up this thing?" he asked, looking over his shoulder at her. "And we have to get up there. I have something for you."

Well, that was good enough incentive. So she backed up and limped his way, taking a flying leap at the last second, jumping onto his back and nearly knocking him over as they both laughed.

But it worked. Soon she was settled and he was making his way up, taking it at an easy pace as Jade kept her arms around him, smiling against his skin as the sun continued its descent.

And then, he stopped, gently lowering her down and taking a breath as he took in the view.

She took it in as well, her breath catching again at the rolling hills, the beauty of the landscape, and the feeling in her heart at finally being here.

China.

"Here," Taylor said, slipping something into her hand. "There's something you need to do while you're here."

She looked down, peering at the silver chain he'd placed there, the pendant attached. A disc with her name engraved on it…

… and a crack down the middle.

"What –" she began to ask as she touched it, just as it broke in half. "Oh, no!"

"No, that's supposed to happen," Taylor said, reaching out and pulling half of the pendant off of the chain. "There's a tradition with a lot of adoptive parents who come to China to get their children. There's a spot on the Great Wall where they leave a lock. And they have two keys. One they throw off the side of the wall and the other they keep. It kind of represents that a piece of their child will always be here in China, no matter where they go." He looked around. "This, however, is not that spot. And what I just gave you isn't a lock. And we're not Mark and Molly, are we?"

"They never made it up here," Jade said, knowing what he was getting at. "They never even made it to Beijing. They spent their time in Shanghai getting me to a doctor there, having him send records over to their doctor in the US…"

They'd been good parents. They *were* good parents. She said a little silent prayer of thanksgiving for Mark and Molly.

And for Taylor, as he smiled at her.

"But it's a good tradition, nonetheless," he said. "And I thought maybe you'd want to leave part of yourself here. A way of celebrating your past in China. Your present in the US. And your future with…"

With me.

He didn't say it, but she heard it anyway.

Oh, how this warmed her heart.

"Yes," she said, letting him put the pendant in her hand. "Put the necklace on me, will you? With the half I'm taking with me."

And he did, his fingers lingering pleasantly on her skin, then resting on her shoulders as she took a breath, looking down at the pendant in her hand…

… right before tossing it over the wall and into the air, watching as the wind picked it up and carried it down, down, down until they could no longer see it.

"Thank you," she said into the silence as she and Taylor watched the sun set, as he wound his arms around her, as she turned to face him at last, her arms around him as well. "Thank you for… for…"

For everything you've done. For being here with me.

For being you, Taylor. God's gift to me beyond China and this season of my life.

For being a part of my forever.

He seemed to understand the words she didn't even utter as he lifted his hands to her face there in the last moments of twilight, smiled at her once again, then put his lips to hers.

And Jade was breathless, all over again.

Bliss.

Every day with Jade was bliss.

It had been before, back before she'd been more to him than a friend, someone he could help, someone who had helped him to find his way back to faith. She'd made every day back then so happy, by just being her.

But now… oh, now the joy felt exponential.

They probably made his parents a little uncomfortable as they spent the next few days in Beijing, staring at one another longingly, with Taylor fighting the need to touch her constantly and only succeeding half of the time. No, he took every opportunity he had to lean down and kiss her, to hold her close, and to whisper to her that he was so thankful for her.

What a surprising thing that God had done in his life this year. He found himself anticipating many years of blessings added onto blessings, now that Jade was in his life, now that she looked at him with stars in her eyes, too.

Stars and apprehension, as they ended their time as tourists in Beijing and headed back to Shanghai. Jade did her best to hide it on that final night with his parents, as they all sat around the dinner table, eating pizza and chatting. It was probably the most that Jade had eaten the whole trip, honestly, and by the end of it all, she was looking a little squeamish.

"Can we pray for you, Jade?" Owen had asked, sensing that the unease had more to do with what was ahead than the food.

"Please," Jade had breathed.

What a gift to hear his parents pray over her much like her own parents had, his mother slipping into Mandarin without realizing what she was doing about halfway through her entreaties that God would use the next few days for His glory, not just in this season but in the seasons to come.

Not just for Jade but for Xiu as well.

Taylor was praying likewise as their flight landed in Chengdu, glancing over to see that Jade was looking even more nervous than she had.

"We don't have to meet her today," he said, just as the plane rolled to a stop. "You can take some time to get your bearings —"

"No, she's expecting us today," Jade had said, shaking her head. "I mean, that's what you told her, right? That we'd visit her today?"

It was. He'd called Xiu from Shanghai, introducing himself on the phone, talking with her like an old friend, which was what she felt like after all the messages he'd translated between her and Jade. He'd put Jade on the phone with her as well after his parents had given them some privacy, but Jade had sat there silently as Xiu had talked and cried, all of her words in Mandarin, of course.

I'm sorry. I'm so sorry. I've missed you every day of your life.

Honored daughter. Precious girl.

Wanted child.

Jade hadn't understood a word, but she'd known the grief even without a translation, tears in her eyes as Taylor had gotten back on the line to discuss with Xiu the details of their Chengdu trip.

She was waiting eagerly, expecting them this afternoon.

Maybe it was too soon. Maybe Jade needed –

"This is why we're here, Taylor," she said, standing up and putting her backpack on. "And I'm… I'm going to be okay."

He'd slipped her hand into his and squeezed, leading her off the plane and through the airport, then to the arrivals lounge, looking around for his brother.

"Oh," he heard Jade breathe before he'd caught sight of the other man himself.

But that one word – and the way she'd said it – let him know that she'd seen the older Robinson brother already.

Hudson.

Yep, sure enough there he was, hands in his pockets, standing a few yards away, smirking.

Hudson was a good looking guy. Better looking than his younger brother – Taylor could admit it – and he was charming in a way that came across without him even saying a word. And then, when he did speak? Well, women lost their minds around him.

Taylor had hated that about him when he was a teenager. He kind of hated it now, too, as he looked back and saw that Jade was blushing.

No matter, though. Hudson was in front of them now, smiling toward Jade and reaching out to punch Taylor on the shoulder.

A little harder than a simple greeting punch.

"Oww," Taylor muttered, punching him back.

Twenty-three and twenty-two and acting like they were still fourteen and thirteen. Their mother would be so proud.

"Hi there," Hudson said to Jade, ignoring Taylor entirely. "I'm Hudson Robinson. You must be Jade."

"Yeah," Jade said, holding her hand out. Hudson took it after a moment's hesitation.

Hudson hadn't been to the US in several years. He'd probably forgotten that this was a thing, shaking hands with people in greeting.

But he was smooth, staring intently at Jade as he took her hand in his and held it there for a long moment.

"You look like her," he said.

Oh, so this wasn't him being smooth. Well, it was. But the staring was because he was seeing the similarities that Taylor hadn't yet gotten to see.

"Like who?" Jade asked, flustered. Then, with realization. "Oh."

"I went by and met her," Hudson said, looking over at Taylor, all flirtation towards Jade on halt as he turned serious. "Like we all talked about. Got her sample. She understood it all, was fine with it. She's a nurse, Taylor."

A nurse. Well, then she'd understood that they were going to do a DNA test immediately, that Hudson was helping out with that, and that one of his genetics professors had agreed to lend his expertise.

But a nurse. If she'd been a nurse back then, back when she'd had Jade, why had she abandoned her? Why – and Taylor was assuming this is how she'd felt, not knowing any different – had she felt helpless with a special needs child if she had medical knowledge?

"She's young, Taylor," Hudson added. "Really young. And…" He smiled at Jade again. "She definitely looks like you. But I'm not sure if that's a family thing or… a people group thing. Wow, Jade. You…"

He saw it, too. What had caught Taylor's eye at first when Jade had told him she was Chinese, that she had been born in Shanghai.

Of course it had been more than that that had taken Taylor's breath away. Hudson's, too, Taylor thought irritably as his brought raised his eyebrow at her.

"Shall we go?" he said, holding his arm out for her gallantly. "Taylor can get the luggage while you and I head on out."

Taylor barely refrained from rolling his eyes.

"We don't have any bags besides these," Jade said, gesturing to their backpacks and moving away from Hudson's arm to take Taylor's hand, snuggling up to his side as she did so.

Take that, Hudson.

But Hudson let it roll off of him.

"Then let's go, huh?"

Hudson was a horrible driver.

Taylor's time in the US had almost been long enough for him to forget about the horror of riding on the back of his brother's motorbike in rush hour Shanghai traffic. But every remembrance came screaming back to him in Chengdu's traffic, as he sat barely squeezed onto the seat behind Hudson, with Jade tucked in between them so that she was the safest.

Three people on a motorbike. People did it all the time here, of course, but it wasn't the safest. And Taylor was almost certain that Hudson was taking the corners and making lane changes even more sporadically than called for, probably trying to throw Taylor off the back.

"We're all in one piece," Hudson said when he got them to his flat, a tiny setup not too far from the medical school where he was studying and only a bit of a drive from the panda base. "Jade, you've got my room, I've got the couch here in the living room, and Taylor…" He looked at his brother. "You get your choice of the floor or the kitchen counter."

"The options are limited here," Taylor said, looking around the small space. "But we appreciate it."

"So much, Hudson," Jade agreed. "Thank you."

"You'll thank me even more in a day or two when I have your results," Hudson said with a grin, moving to the kitchen. "Let me just get my bag of magic."

"Bag of magic?" Jade whispered when he was out of view.

"Don't ask me," Taylor said. "Hudson's a weird freak."

And I'm so glad that you weren't charmed by him like so many other women, he almost added.

Jade heard it anyway, stepping up to him with a smile and pulling his face down to hers, kissing him tenderly.

"Get a room," Hudson said loudly, coming back in with a bag in his arms. "Or not, since we don't have any more here, as I've already mentioned."

"What's that?" Taylor asked, eyeing the load in his brother's arms.

"My bag of magic," Hudson said with a sigh. "I've already got Xiu's blood. I just need Jade's now."

"Are you qualified to take someone's blood?" Taylor asked, doubting this very much.

"More than qualified," Hudson reassured him. "Jade, I do this all the time."

As a first year medical student?

"Okay," Jade said, agreeable to it, already cinching up her sleeve as Hudson rummaged around in his bag.

"I'm not sure," Taylor cut in, not trusting his brother. "Can we go somewhere to do this, somewhere that —"

"I'll practice on Taylor," Hudson said, ignoring him and grinning roguishly at Jade as he pulled out an enormous syringe and brandished it wildly in the air. "Already took my own blood earlier, and I'll use his sample and mine to compare and contrast, just so I'll know what I'm looking at."

"What?" Taylor asked.

"Going to do our DNA, too, just for fun!" Hudson said, moving towards him. "I'll get yours first. Then Jade's."

"I thought you were going to have a professional do Jade's," Taylor protested, even as Hudson raised up his sleeve. "That you were going to have one of your professors look at Jade's sample and her mother's —"

"Oh, I will," Hudson said, holding the syringe aloft, ready. "I'm going to take her sample, but I'm going to let my professor compare hers and Xiu's. I'm not going to take chances with that. No way. There will be a legit geneticist who will assess her results, not just a med student. So you can trust them — they'll be correct. But I'm going to have fun observing and trying my hand at our samples, brother."

And with that, he jabbed the needle right into Taylor's arm.

Taylor swore loudly in Mandarin, attempting to jerk away from his brother.

"Dude, you need to wash your mouth out with soap," Hudson said, putting him in a headlock. "And stay put, unless you want to make this worse. You've got a ginormous needle in your arm!"

"Hudson!" Taylor bellowed. "You didn't even warn me or sanitize anything or —"

"Just a practice run," Hudson said. "Wow, stings a little, doesn't it? But that's because we're not as fat as pandas, don't have as much fur to get through, you know? Probably should have used human needles on us, not these gigantic ones made for large mammals, but I couldn't resist –"

"Good grief," Taylor managed, close to tears.

"Don't you worry, Jade," Hudson said with a grin. "I saved the smaller needles for you, along with the alcohol swabs, and the gloves I'll be wearing when I do yours."

"I appreciate that," Jade said, just as Hudson finally finished up with Taylor's arm.

"Ugh," Taylor kept groaning.

"Good grief, man," Hudson said, capping off his brother's sample and disposing of all that he'd used. "Grow a pair."

Taylor frowned at him. "Watch your words."

"Oh," Hudson said, turning to Jade with a grimace. "Sorry about that."

"You're good," Jade said, smiling at them both, trying to hold back her laughter. "And I'm ready when you are."

Hudson was better to Jade, taking his time, wearing gloves, sanitizing her arm, and actually using a normal needle.

"See, that?" Hudson said, throwing the words over to Taylor. "You need to grow a pair like Jade."

"Hudson," Taylor said again, warning in his voice.

"And you're good," Hudson said, finishing up with her. "And I'll get this to my professor. He said he'd get right on it, so I'm hopeful that you'll know for sure by the time the two of you leave Chengdu."

They would know for sure. But hadn't they already assumed they did, to the point of regarding it as a certainty?

And Hudson's response when he'd seen Jade… hadn't that confirmed it further?

"I borrowed a friend's bike for you," Hudson said to Taylor now. "Figured that way you and Jade could be free to go and do as you need to."

"I appreciate that," Taylor said.

Beyond the annoyances he could feel with his brother, he did appreciate everything he'd done, everything he was going to do.

Especially as he held Jade's blood sample and communicated something silently with Taylor, their eyes meeting.

It's all going to work out.

Taylor hoped so.

And only minutes later, as Jade was holding onto him and he was driving through the streets of Chengdu, right to the address Xiu had given him weeks ago, he prayed it so.

Lord, be with us.

Be with Jade.

~Jade~

It was like a dream.

Standing here, at this door, to this small apartment tucked away into a building on a side street in Chengdu, where the sounds of traffic and busy Chinese life fell away.

Or maybe it just fell away for Jade, who took a deep breath, readying herself for this moment.

She was going to meet her birth mother. Her real mother.

She'd made it here. Despite all the impossible odds and the roadblocks, she'd made it here, where she would meet the woman who had given birth to her, who had abandoned her.

Yet she was hesitant, looking at the door.

"You okay?" Taylor asked softly.

No. Not really.

"I will be," she whispered.

And after a few more breaths, she nodded at him.

"Okay," he murmured, taking a deep breath himself. "Here we go."

He reached out and knocked on the door, stepping back and shoving his hands into his pockets nervously. Then, thinking better of it, he pulled his hands back out, reaching for Jade's and lacing his fingers through hers with a squeeze.

Praise God for Taylor, here with her in this huge moment.

The thanksgiving was the last thought she had before the door opened.

Jade felt her breath catch again, and her heart… oh, her heart stilled for a moment, then began to pound.

There she was. A woman. A very young woman. Standing there, her hands dropping from the door and covering her mouth.

Covering half of her face did nothing to hide her resemblance to Jade, though. Jade had hardly been able to take it all in, to take in another breath, before Xiu was reaching out to her and pulling her into her arms.

And then the words came. Mandarin words, accompanied by sobs. Heaving, emotional sobs, making it impossible for Taylor to translate it well.

"I'm sorry, I'm sorry," he said. "She's telling you that she's sorry, Jade."

Jade nodded, blinking back her own tears, as Xiu held onto her, still continuing to sob.

And it was a haze from there, to Xiu holding her face in her hands and smiling through the tears, to Xiu leading them both into her home, to Xiu preparing tea for them, to Jade looking around and wondering why she'd never thought to have Taylor ask about Xiu's family, about a husband, about other children.

Jade could have brothers and sisters. It was possible, wasn't it?

And it was too much to comprehend.

But Xiu noticed her perusal, in between the small talk she was making with Taylor, clearly as nervous and uncertain as Jade was.

She began to talk. Jade wished for the hundredth or more time this trip alone that she could understand, that she could speak Mandarin as well.

"She says that she lives by herself," Taylor said. "That her apartment is just the right size for one person."

"Oh," Jade said, nodding and attempting a smile. "Tell her that it's a nice home."

And it was. Jade imagined briefly what it would have been like to have grown up here with a single mother.

Had Xiu been single when she'd become a mother?

Xiu smiled as Taylor translated the compliment.

And then, she cleared her throat nervously, looking to Jade again but speaking to Taylor.

"She says that you must have questions," he said. "And she wants to answer them all."

All the answers she could have ever wanted, here for her right now.

Where would she even begin?

"I want to know her story," Jade said softly. "My story."

Was that sufficient? She wondered as Taylor translated the words and as Xiu nodded.

And then, she began to tell them.

"She was eighteen, in her first year of university," he began. "Here in Chengdu. She left her home in the country to come here to get medical training. She wanted to go back to her own people and do medical work in her village."

Eighteen. A university student, studying in a medical field. Just like Jade. She'd probably looked just like Jade as well. And Jade began to picture it in her mind, even as she raised her eyes and watched Xiu as she struggled to tell the story.

"She met your father at the university," he said as Xiu continued on, fidgeting in her seat. "He was a… he was a professor."

Jade fought to keep her expression neutral. It would do no good to reveal her emotions at this point when there were so many other difficult revelations still ahead.

But Xiu looked ashamed even still.

"He was a visiting professor from overseas," Taylor said, continuing to translate. "Here in Chengdu on a fellowship. He was… Australian?"

At this, Jade couldn't stop herself from looking to him with confusion.

"He… what?"

Taylor shook his head and spoke to Xiu, looking for clarification as he spoke quickly in Mandarin. She responded, and he took a breath.

"Yeah… Australian." He looked at Jade. "Which would… well, that would explain even further why you don't look like everyone else."

Yes, it would.

Australian. What a weird turn.

"He was married," Taylor translated as Xiu continued on, an even deeper look of shame on her face as she gave this piece of information. "And he made it clear that he was done when she found out that she was pregnant. As did her parents. Her father – your grandfather – is an important man in the village. And this was a disgrace. They disowned her."

Eighteen. On her own.

Pregnant.

Unfathomable.

"She had you, though," Taylor continued on. "Quit university to earn money, to save up for the future. She wanted you, Jade."

Wanted you. Past tense. Wanted you until she discovered that you weren't perfect.

Jade did her best to dismiss the bitter thought, looking back at Xiu, seeing that the older woman was fighting back tears as she continued.

"And you were born," Taylor said. "The delivery went well, but the newborn days… they were difficult. Something wasn't right from the beginning. She could tell. You weren't well, weren't thriving like babies are supposed to. You weren't putting on weight. And as time went on, it became very clear that… well, that you needed more medical attention."

At this, Xiu began to cry again.

"She didn't know what she was doing. Didn't know that there was help out there for children like you, even for mothers who had no money. She didn't know that she could get help. And you were so sick…"

Jade could feel the desperation in this. Even though her heart was conflicted, she could feel the agony of this predicament, of being left to feel as though you had no alternatives. She reached out and put her hand in Xiu's.

And that was enough encouragement for Xiu to continue on.

"She knew of a place," he said. "A place where you could leave a baby."

There was apology in Xiu's eyes as they locked onto Jade's. And what was Jade supposed to do with that? Tell her it wasn't okay, that it would never be okay?

She just nodded in understanding, willing her to go on.

"So she did," Taylor continued translating. "And then, she threw herself back into her studies to forget what she'd done. But the more she learned, the more she realized that she could have done more. And she's regretted it – regretted giving you up – every day since. She never married, never had more children. She's been waiting and hoping…"

For this.

Jade looked at Xiu, hearing and understanding every last word. But still… oh, still…

She swallowed.

"I understand," she said softly. "I understand."

It wasn't forgiveness, but it was a start.

And it was enough for Xiu, who embraced her and began crying again in earnest.

~Taylor~

Surreal. It was all surreal.

Jade and Xiu, sitting on the couch together, like a past and present version of the same woman. He was catching each word, translating it as best as he could, yet still sitting as a spectator to it all.

Honored daughter. Precious girl.

Wanted child.

Xiu had said it more than once as she'd told them her story, along with this endearment – *my American daughter*. And she'd determined early on that Taylor was more than just a translator, calling him her Chinese son.

That had lightened the mood a lot, enough that by the early evening, they'd all felt like they'd survived a day of walking through emotional mine fields. Enough that they were able to make plans for the next day, for an outing together, bonding time, helpfully arranged by Hudson.

Taylor was thankful for his brother's help, for the car that he arranged to come and pick them up from Xiu's apartment early the next day, for the chatty driver who took them out to the panda center, and for the easy stroll that Xiu, Jade, and Taylor were able to take at Jade's pace through the enclosures.

"Baby pandas," Jade had cooed as they'd stood in front of the glass that protected the nursery, looking at the tiny, pink cubs resting in incubators.

"Your brother told me that he works here," Xiu had said to Taylor in Mandarin.

"He shovels poop," Taylor had said back to her with a grin.

And Xiu had laughed. Wow, that had taken his breath away because he could hear Jade's laugh in the sound.

He'd exchanged a look with Jade, noting that she, too, had heard it.

Then, Xiu had spoken again, smiling at him.

"What did she say?" Jade asked when Taylor blushed.

"She said that Hudson and I are respectful boys," he translated. "Handsome, too. She wanted you to know that either one of us would be a great catch."

"Well, tell her that I've already made my choice," Jade said, lifting up on her toes to kiss him on the cheek.

Xiu had smiled at this as well. Xiu had been smiling all day, in fact, through lunch and the early afternoon, then as evening drew near, as they drove back into Chengdu and she took them on a walking tour of her part of the city, showing them the hospital where she worked, explaining that she'd gone for further schooling so as to specialize in pediatrics, working with children with conditions just like Jade's.

Jade had been emotional about this and as they'd taken a taxi to one more spot that Xiu wanted to show them before they said goodnight.

Taylor knew exactly where they were as soon as they stopped, recognizing the street name on the app he'd had running, tracking where they were going so that he'd be able to map it all out for himself later, for Jade, for the trips they would make in the future.

They were on the same street where Jade had been left as an infant. He had the address, was ready to turn right as he stepped out of the cab —

But Xiu turned to the left.

Wait… where was she going? He thought it as she and Jade walked together hand in hand, farther and farther away from where the orphanage had once been.

And then, he stopped abruptly, just as they did, just as Xiu stopped in front of an unfamiliar building.

There was something wrong with this. Taylor thought it to himself, as Xiu stood with Jade, hand in hand, as Xiu spoke.

"She says this is the place where she left you," he translated, knowing even as he said it that it couldn't be right.

But the anguish on Xiu's face as she turned to Jade in this very spot spoke to the truth of it. This was where she'd put her infant, this is where she'd given her up, this is where she'd lost a piece of herself.

This was the spot…

… but this wasn't the spot where Jade had been left.

Same street, yes. But this was a medical clinic. Taylor took in the words. Had something been lost in translation in the inquiry? Or had it been different back then, a state-run orphanage, the very one where Jade had been left?

No. That hadn't been here, it had been down the street, at least ten blocks away.

Right?

There was doubt here. Plausible doubt, on Taylor's part at least.

But there was none on Xiu's as she took Jade's face in her hands and wept, leaning her forehead onto the younger woman's, closing her eyes, and moaning her plea.

Forgive me, honored daughter, precious girl, wanted child.

He translated it again and saw the conflict on Jade's face.

Did she know that the address wasn't quite right?

No, that wasn't it, as she, too closed her eyes and wept, clinging tighter to Xiu.

And Taylor chose to stay quiet about it all, as mother and child mourned together.

~Jade~

Dissatisfied.

Every hope that Jade had when she'd started the search for her mother had been met. They'd found her even with impossible odds. And not only had they found her, they'd gone to China, connected with her, had stood with her in the very place where she'd left Jade years ago.

But Jade was still dissatisfied.

Oh, Lord, help me, she prayed as she and Taylor made their way away from Xiu's apartment, as she leaned her cheek against Taylor's back as he navigated the borrowed motorbike through Chengdu's nighttime traffic.

Help me to be okay.

She was still wrestling with it as they sat together at a local restaurant, their meals laid out before them. Jade was picking at hers, but it had nothing to do with the food.

"Big day," Taylor murmured, understanding in his voice.

Understatement. Wow.

"Are you okay?"

She wasn't.

"I'm struggling," she said honestly.

She could be honest with him, could be honest with these ugly feelings she was having.

"I wanted her to have to give an answer for what she did," she said, scarcely able to get the words out. "A better answer than what she gave. Because no matter what she was going through, what she felt, what she thought she could do at the time…"

She swallowed. She understood what Xiu had done, why she'd done it.

But…

"It wasn't right," Jade said. "Leaving me like that. Leaving me at the back door of some orphanage and walking away forever. Leaving me. Like I was unwanted."

Taylor nodded patiently, no judgment in his gaze.

"I get that," he said. "And I get that you needed an answer. Or maybe not needed it as much as… well, wanted that justice. Wanted your birth mother to own what she'd done. To pay for it."

Justice. Retribution.

Jade couldn't believe that she felt these things. But they'd been there all along, somewhere deep in her heart, looking for someone to blame for the way she'd always struggled with feeling unwanted.

"But let me ask you this," Taylor said tenderly.

And it was the tenderness in his voice that made her heart ache, knowing what words were coming, knowing the grace that Taylor had experienced, the grace that had transformed him over the last few months.

Grace…

"Yes?" she asked weakly.

"When you look at Xiu," he said, that name passing through his lips with such gentleness, with the same kind of gentleness in Xiu's own touch and smile and words and tears. "When you look at her, do you want justice for what was done to you? Do you want her to give an answer beyond what she's already given?"

Beyond the tears that had soaked Jade's shirt? Beyond the almost inhuman sobs Xiu had given as she'd embraced her lost child? Beyond the grief that was so much deeper and graver than Jade could ever fathom feeling?

No. Please, Jesus, no. Give Xiu grace. Give her grace that won't call for an answer to her mistake but will give healing to her sorrow.

This was so hard. So, so hard…

And Jade didn't even have to say it out loud. Taylor was there with her, sliding into the seat next to her, his arm around her, his lips to her temple.

"I'm sorry, Jade," he murmured. "I'm so sorry…"

~Taylor~

"It… what?"

Taylor shook his head at the words, his mind rushing with all that had happened, with what he'd just heard.

He and Jade had come back from dinner, and he'd rejoiced to see that she was smiling again. That likely had nothing to do with the stress of the past two days, of the heartache and joy combined in meeting her mother, but everything to do with Taylor downloading a Chinese movie to his phone and watching it with her, rushing to translate everything and failing in the process, so much so that neither one of them knew what was going on with the plot, the characters – none of it.

Lost in translation. Times ten thousand.

"You need to learn Mandarin," he'd said. "For real."

"I will eventually," she'd said, giving him a goodnight kiss. "Because tomorrow… it won't be our last day here."

It would be for this trip but not forever.

"I need to try calling Mom again," she'd said, looking at her phone. "We keep playing phone tag. I think she's gotten the time difference screwed up, even with that clock you gave her that has both times on it."

She'd been so excited about that clock – to the point of tears – but she'd likely confused the am and pm times and was totally lost now.

"Poor Molly," he'd laughed.

And Jade had kissed him one last time then headed on to bed.

But he'd stayed up, watching the movie by himself until Hudson came back home, his expression troubled, the words he'd given Taylor even more troubling.

"It wasn't a match."

That's what Taylor thought his brother had said.

"Xiu and Jade's DNA doesn't match?" he asked carefully, needing to know for sure.

"No," Hudson said softly.

Taylor felt the breath rush from his lungs, remembering the look in Jade's eyes as she'd spent the day with Xiu in the city, as there had been real happiness in her smile during some of those sweet moments. Conflict, yes, as there likely would be for a long time, but there was happiness as well.

And now…

"Xiu isn't Jade's mother?" he asked.

"I had my professor check and double check," Hudson said. "So much so that I think he was offended. But he said that he's certain that they're not a match."

Taylor's head dropped into his hands.

"But we're brothers," Hudson said. "Our DNA looked so similar that there was no doubt of that. So there's that."

Little comfort in that, Taylor thought, even as Hudson put his hand to his back and give him a gentle shake, empathy in the motion.

Maybe that was a comfort, though, he thought, looking up at his brother.

"It sucks, man," Hudson said softly. "I mean, not that part about us being brothers. Well, I don't know. That does suck at times as well."

"Yeah," Taylor gave a little laugh that held no humor.

"It sucks for Jade," Hudson said. "Because the search…"

Was for nothing. Would end here because they'd done all they could.

They'd only found Xiu. A woman who didn't share Jade's DNA. A woman who had been broken because of her lost child.

A woman who wanted Jade to be her daughter with everything in her.

"She took us to the wrong spot," Taylor said.

"What spot?"

"The spot where she dropped off her baby," Taylor said. "It was really close to where Jade was found, but… it wasn't exactly right. So I wondered. But I'd hoped that maybe things had changed, maybe Xiu hadn't gotten it right… I'd just hoped that I was wrong."

Hudson let out a deep breath as well. "What were the odds? You know? That their stories are so similar, that they look so much alike —"

"That China is so huge that there must be thousands of stories just like Jade's," Taylor finished for him.

"That's true," Hudson said thoughtfully. "But still… this sucks."

Yes. Yes, it did.

"What are you going to tell Jade?" he asked.

The truth. What else was there to tell?

Hudson seemed to get it.

"Then I'll be praying for you," he said.

And Taylor nodded, appreciative of this.

He didn't wait for the morning.

He went into Hudson's room where Jade was already asleep and woke her up, gently and tenderly, sitting with her on the bed as she rubbed her eyes and turned on the lamp.

And then, he told her.

There were questions, tears, and then…

"So somewhere out there," Jade said softly, "there's a young woman just about my age. One who likely has cerebral palsy as well. One who was adopted and who is living a life somewhere far away from China, likely not even giving her birth parents a second thought, not knowing how her mother wept over me at even the possibility that I…"

She shook her head, unable to keep the tears at bay now.

"That you were hers," Taylor said, tenderly, gently. "That you were every hope and prayer that she'd been whispering in her heart over the last eighteen years."

"Yeah, that," Jade managed. "But I wasn't. I wasn't any of those things. I wasn't hers. And who even knows…"

Where I came from. Who I belonged to. What my life would have been.

Taylor could hear her thinking it. And he could see her chiding herself for feeling what she felt, when the greater tragedy just might possibly be that Xiu, who had finally atoned for what she'd done because she'd been able to hold Jade in her arms and apologize, might have to feel the loss all over again.

"What do I tell her?" Jade barely managed. "What do I tell her about this?"

Taylor said nothing for a long moment, choosing his words carefully, knowing that there were no easy answers.

But there was truth. And there was grace.

"I think you should tell her," he said. "Right before you tell her that nothing has changed, and that you'll be her American daughter."

Jade turned to him, the tears escaping from her eyes again.

"And I'll be her Chinese son," he said, shrugging slightly, smiling at her.

"Taylor," she said, reaching out for him.

And he kissed her hands, feeling a rush of even greater affection for her in this moment, remembering how well she'd loved and comforted Xiu, no doubt praying all the while as she'd done so, knowing that God had directed all of their steps to one another, even though her heart was conflicted and hurting.

God had directed them there. No doubt. But still…

"No matter what happens with finding your birth mother," he said carefully, his words slow and sure, his eyes on her now, "you can rest in this, Jade. You're wanted. By your mom and dad. By Xiu. By God, of course."

Wanted.

"And by me," he said, his voice softer now, so vulnerable. "I want you, Jade. Forever."

There were no easy answers in any of this.

But she could trust this. That she was wanted, that he wanted her, would always want her.

Forever.

And as she put her hands to his face, her lips to his, he rejoiced that she could count on this promise.

~Jade~

She didn't tell Xiu.

She'd been prepared to let her know about the DNA test, explaining how there wasn't enough evidence there for a positive connection, something that Hudson had told Taylor meant a definitive no when it came to establishing Xiu and Jade as mother and child.

Yes, Xiu had left her baby in Chengdu at around the same time that Jade had been left, and, yes, their physical similarities were striking. But it wasn't so different than many of the women Jade saw and met as she and Taylor had spent time in this corner of China, where Jade had seen that what she thought was clear proof that she was Xiu's daughter was nothing more than just being among her own people group for the first time in her life.

And as far as the date that Xiu had confidently told her as her birthdate – a gift to Jade at the time – that date was likely someone else's birthdate.

There was another child somewhere out there. Jade had been ready to tell Xiu that, to assure her that there was still hope that she would know her child one day –

But she'd been unable to say a single one of those words, unable to imagine Taylor translating them, when Xiu had embraced her at the door with that dazzling smile and the words that fell from her lips.

Honored daughter. Precious girl.

Wanted child.

There would be no further heartbreak for Xiu, not if Jade could help it. And though Taylor exchanged a concerned look with her at first as she went on as though nothing had changed, eventually he, too, looked resigned and resolved, spending the day with Xiu, promising her that they would return one day soon, and kissing her goodbye warmly, her good Chinese son.

Jade cried all the way back to the airport, not relenting as Hudson hugged her goodbye and did his best to reassure her, telling her that he'd check in on Xiu when he could. She was still crying as Taylor led her through security, as he found the gate for their flight to Shanghai, and as he claimed seats for them in the crowded terminal, their tickets in his hand.

It was only when he was sitting next to her, only when she put her arm through his and laid her head on his shoulder, that her tears subsided.

"You didn't tell her," he said softly.

"Was I wrong not to?" she asked, still not sure if she'd done the right thing.

"I don't know," he said honestly.

"Will her real daughter find her one day?" Jade asked. "And my mother…"

My mother, my real mother, somewhere in China…

"I don't know, Jade," Taylor said again, leaning over and placing a kiss on her head. "And your real mother –"

Her phone began ringing, cutting him off. Jade wiped at her eyes and dug around in her backpack for it, shooting him an apologetic look.

"Take it," he said. "And I'll go and grab you something to drink, okay?"

She nodded even as she brought the phone to her ear, taking a deep breath as she did so.

"Hello?"

"Jade!"

It was Molly, sounding very excited, concerned, and emotional, all with just that one word.

Jade.

"Mom," Jade sighed, feeling herself getting choked up again. While Taylor was amazing and was quickly becoming her safe place in this uncertain season in her life, there was something comforting about hearing her mother's voice, a security in knowing that Molly would understand how much this all hurt and how exhilarating it was all at the same time, Molly who would cry or rejoice with her, Molly who would want the best for her, no matter the cost to herself.

"Jade, I've been praying," Molly said, blubbering the words. "I kept getting the times screwed up! That clock Taylor got me was perfect, of course, but I confused the am times for the pm times! And I missed your call, baby. But I've been praying and waiting and thinking about you and… oh, Jade, was she wonderful? What a gift for her, knowing you, Jade…"

And Molly was weeping again.

"Mom," Jade said, her voice tremulous. "It's okay…"

"I'm just happy," Molly sobbed, desperately attempting to get herself under control, judging by the gasps and heavy breaths. "I'm so happy that you found her. That she found you! And that she was able to know that no matter how hard it was all those years ago to do what she felt she had to do… well, that you are still amazing, still wonderful, still incredible, still my perfect Jade. That you've brought so much happiness to me, every day since I first held you in my arms."

Wanted. So wanted.

"How much more happiness must you have brought to her?" she continued on, true joy in her voice now. "By finding her, by going so far to get to her… And for you, Jade. Was it amazing, being with your real mother?"

My real mother. Jade had the thought again, the tears spilling down her face.

Her real mother, an ocean away.

I love you, Jade. You are so loved and so wanted.

Oh, Molly had whispered the words over her so many years ago, and every day since had been a testament to the truth of it. And even now, even an ocean away, Molly was still loving her, still laying herself down for the daughter of her heart, wanting nothing but the best for her child.

You've brought so much happiness to me, every day since I first held you in my arms.

Wanted. Always and forever.

Jade smiled to herself through her tears, as Molly continued to ask questions, as she continued to want to know all the details, as she was being supportive and encouraging and loving, just as she'd always been.

My *real* mother.

She'd had that all along. And while she'd known it her whole life, it took going to China, where it all began, to know it in a new way.

Thank You, God, for my mother.

"Mom," Jade cut in with a laugh and a sob, all rolled into one. "I love you."

And Molly sighed as well.

"And I love you, Jade," she said, tears in her voice. "Always have and always will."

Christmas is different this year.

I smile as my heart affirms it, as my eyes take in the scene before me, and as her hand finds mine.

It's a little hand, tiny and warm… and sticky. I have Xiu to thank for that, I think with a chuckle, as I look down to find that Lynn's mouth is full of the same sweet Chinese treat that covers her hands. I don't know when Xiu slipped it to her, if it was within the last few minutes or if it was when we arrived on the night train from Shanghai, when she burst into tears at the sight of the five of us – Jade, Lynn, Mark, Molly, and me – standing outside her door.

Well, six of us. Jade was able to tell Xiu, in her own very basic, very tentative Mandarin, that we're expecting again, saying the words again in English as well so that her parents would also hear the news. And when Xiu and Molly exploded with more tears and so many questions and exclamations, hugging one another gleefully, not understanding one another's words in the slightest but understanding the sentiment entirely, Jade just smiled at me, tears in her own eyes, as she laughed out loud.

Oh, one day she will understand Xiu better. I can fill in the blanks until then, and I do, speaking with her often whether in China or stateside, caring for and bringing honor to my Chinese mother.

I'm not the only one. My parents visit Xiu often, and my mother, more Chinese than American after all these years she's loved this place, has been a friend and a confidante to Xiu during the past few years. She's family, after all, and they both believe – without anyone to argue with them – that their granddaughter, Lynn, is the most perfect child ever born.

Their granddaughter.

Being a family is about much more than genetics, than biology, than blood. Jade and I know it well, knew it all those years ago when we got back to Shanghai on that hard morning after we left Xiu for the first time. We knew it when Hudson called me, breathless.

"I found out something," he'd said, urgency in his tone. "Please tell me that Jade hasn't told Xiu about the DNA test."

"She hasn't," I'd said, hope in my heart as I'd lowered my voice, not wanting Jade to be hurt any further. "Was it wrong?"

"No, it was right," Hudson said. "Xiu's not Jade's mother."

Then why had he been calling?

"I couldn't get Xiu's story out of my mind," he'd kept on. "She told it all to me on the day I got her sample. And then you told me about the address, where she dropped her child –"

"What does this have to do with Jade?" I'd asked, hearing nothing but the simple truth in Hudson's words. Xiu wasn't Jade's mother. What more mattered?

"I don't want Jade to tell Xiu that they weren't a match," Hudson had said, true concern in his voice. "I don't want Xiu to continue to search for her unborn child because…"

There had been a long silence.

"Hudson, tell me," I had said.

And the story had come out, about how Hudson had made some calls, done some research, chatted up some of his connections at the government offices in Chengdu. Hudson knew Chengdu, had charmed so many people, and was able to get doors opened that Xiu hadn't, likely because she'd not known where to go, who to speak to, or where to find her information.

"Did you find her daughter?" I asked, leaping ahead of Hudson's explanation. "How is that even possible?! It took us months to even find a possible lead for Jade –"

"Because there was no documentation involved with abandoning a child," Hudson had interrupted me. "Jade's mother didn't sign anything, didn't identify herself. These babies that are dropped off – it's nearly impossible for them to find the women who left them." He'd breathed deeply. "But finding babies? Much simpler. And I'm glad I didn't tell Xiu any of that when I met her."

Why, though?

"Taylor," Hudson said softly. "I found the documentation for Xiu's baby. The drop off location. The birthdate. The medical condition. Everything was right."

"Where is she?" I asked. "Hudson, you have to tell her, tell Xiu, tell them both that –"

"She died," Hudson said wearily "Just a week after Xiu left her. It was more than cerebral palsy. There were heart issues. And I just… I couldn't bear the thought of Xiu finding out, so I'd hoped…"

That Jade would fill in, would be Xiu's daughter, and would never let Xiu know any different.

I had hoped it as well, but when I'd told Jade, she'd shaken her head, telling me that we needed to call Xiu, that she should have told her about the test, that now she had to tell her the whole truth, the hard truth.

So we'd called, and Jade had told her with me translating, the two of us sharing the phone, our heads close together. And Xiu's grief had needed no translation, nor had Jade's tears as she'd listened to her mourn, loving a child who was no more.

And I myself had been overcome with emotion when Jade had said what she did to Xiu.

"I will be your daughter," she'd said, with love and tenderness and so much grace in her voice, even through her tears. "I am your daughter now. Not in my blood but in my heart. Your daughter, always and forever."

And she has been. And I've been Xiu's son.

And God has been so very good to us all.

I smile at the thought and at the laugh coming from Molly as she wipes at her eyes, laughing at her own attempt to wish Xiu a merry Christmas. I taught her the Mandarin phrase before we came, knowing she wouldn't get it exactly right. But she's tried, and it only endears her more to Xiu. Xiu, who is loved by the Matthews as much as I am, as much as I was long before the day that they gave their blessing for me to marry Jade.

"I want to marry you," I'd whispered to her on our last night in China on that trip years ago, stopping her during our walk along the Bund, all the lights of Shanghai fading to nothing before me as all I saw was Jade. Jade, who'd made the comment more than once in China that she was just one of a million women who looked just like she did, that for the first time in her life she felt nearly invisible.

But she wasn't, because she was walking around with the foreign, Mandarin-speaking white dude.

That and she was Jade. I'd had the thought there in Shanghai as she'd looked up at me, pulling her hair back from her face as the wind blew softly off the Huangpu River, as all around us thousands of people moved, lived, and existed in this one place.

All I could see was Jade.

How could she ever be one of millions when she was the only woman I'd ever see?

"I want to marry you," I'd whispered to her, wrapping my arms around her.

"That's crazy," she'd whispered back, snuggling into me contentedly, the night lights shining in her eyes as she looked up and met my gaze.

"We've said a lot of crazy things here lately," I said, laughing. "About coming back here soon. About making so many trips to China. About seeing different cities next time. About making this home one day."

"Crazy ideas, all of them," she agreed, grinning. "But yes, Taylor. Yes to all of them."

"To all of them?" I asked, smiling as well. And then, considering what she'd said. "Wait… you would marry me?"

"That's crazy," she said again, her hand to her mouth as she laughed. "But yes. I would."

"Totally crazy," I said, laughing out loud with her.

She was young. I was young. We'd only known one another for what amounted to a semester.

But it was decided there in Shanghai, as she'd laughed and I'd laughed, until I leaned down and kissed her, holding her tight, praising God for everything that He'd done in our lives so far and all that He was going to do.

We made it official six months later, back in Jade's hometown in the States, and though our church was filled to the brim on that hot summer day, I hardly noticed anyone but her as she made her way down the aisle to me, sure-footed and certain, a twinkle in her eyes and a smile on her lips.

And it was bliss, every day together from then on. We were poor. So poor as Jade continued with her undergraduate work, fast tracking it all so that she could speed along to the days of applying to pharmacy schools. I was making a slim living playing rare gigs and events in our small community, sometimes driving hours for jobs that would lead to better exposure and more opportunities, with Jade always there beside me. We were happy in the poorest of days, so blissfully happy to be together, to be serving God in our church, and to be looking towards the future together. Then, when Jade was accepted into a pharmacy school in Houston, our lives changed. My opportunities for work transformed drastically, with steady work as a studio musician on top of all the jobs I was able to get for special events. And when we joined the church in the

Chinese community in Houston – the very same church I had grown up in – it opened the door to distinctly cultural opportunities for me, both to play music in a paid position at our church and as the only erhu and yueqin player for any number of Chinese celebrations across the city.

And Jade, for the first time in her life, got to be part of a Chinese family of faith.

"Taylor, a little help?" Jade gestures for me to join her, Xiu, and Molly on the floor, as Mark reaches into his bag. I go and sit with them as well, Lynn in my lap, smiling as she climbs away from me to sit between her grandmothers, as they both squeeze her little hands in their own.

And Jade comes and takes the space beside me, sliding up underneath my arm like she was made to fit here.

"Dad's about to tell the Christmas story," she says, her eyes meeting mine, her lips curling into a beautiful smile. "And we need you to translate for Xiu."

This is our first Christmas with Xiu. Not our first visit here – no – as we've made many trips back over the years, some with Mark and Molly as well, so that Jade could do short term studies in Chinese medicine to add to her pharmaceutical education. There's a client base back home in Houston that can appreciate this and does, and Jade rejoices in how she's able in this way to be a bridge from her past to her present.

And her future? Well, who knows. We may stay in Houston. Or one day, we might find ourselves here in Chengdu, close to Hudson and his family. Or in Shanghai, close to my parents.

Or somewhere we haven't even considered yet.

Jade smiles at me as Mark begins the story, a familiar one to our hearts.

The possibilities for the future are endless. Because of who we serve. Because of who loves us. Because we're wanted by a loving God, who changes us and equips us and gives us purpose.

We're wanted.

"For unto us a child is born," Mark says, and I can see him blink back tears, thinking not just of a child in Bethlehem but of one in Chengdu, of how the world has changed for Xiu and for the Matthews family because of one child, because one child has united them into a family.

And as I begin to translate the words into Mandarin, I think about how God has done so much because of Jade and how it is nothing compared to what He has done through Christ.

Oh, that Xiu would know it. Oh, that we would know it. Oh, that these earthly words would have an eternal impact.

I can feel the amen in the way that Jade squeezes my hand and wipes a tear from her eyes.

Thank You, God, that this is only the beginning of our story…

ABOUT THE AUTHOR

Jenn Faulk is a native Texan who enjoys reading and writing chick lit. She's a pastor's wife, a stay-at-home mom, and a marathon enthusiast who loves talking about Jesus and what a difference He's made in her life. She has a BA in Creative Writing from the University of Houston and a MA in Missiology from Southwestern Baptist Theological Seminary.

For a complete list of all of Jenn's books, visit her website…

www.jennfaulk.com

To connect with Jenn, visit her on Facebook (jennfaulkbooks), Instagram (@jennfaulkbooks), and follow her on Amazon, Bookbub, and Goodreads.